‘AS I WAS A-SAYING’

‘AS I WAS A-SAYING’

Country goings-on

Roger Anthony Freeman

MALTHOUSE PRESS
1993

First published by Malthouse Press, 1993

ISBN 0 9522355 1 X

British Library Cataloguing in Publication Data
A catalogue record for this book is
available from the British Library

Cover by Norman Ottaway

Illustrations by Mark Guthrie

Typeset by
C.B.S.
155 Hamilton Road, Felixstowe, Suffolk

Printed in Great Britain by
Ipswich Book Company Ltd,
The Drift, Nacton Road, Ipswich, Suffolk

Contents

Preface

A COMMON tendency among those of advanced years is to regale others with accounts of the past, partly to indulge in nostalgia and partly because they believe their knowledge and experiences are worth perpetuating. In my youth I knew many an ageing country story-teller who could entertain for hours with memories of people and events, no doubt flavoured with varying degrees of exaggeration and imagination to add piquancy or pungency to the yarns. One was a remarkable sage named Horace Ellis who invariably began his narrations with 'I mind the time . . .' I borrowed this for the title of my first book of humorous country tales and, as this second collection is concerned with the same scene, many of the same characters, and recalled in similar vein, it is a case of 'As I was a-saying.'

Roger Anthony Freeman

An Eye on the Inevitable

Many a farmer would agree that he does not run his farm; the farm runs him. An agricultural businessman may be able to view a farm in purely detached, commercial terms; raw material that must produce a profit. Not the true farmer. He knows that the land both gives and takes; that the more hours of toil and mental concern put into producing crops and livestock, the more one becomes tied to that patch of countryside. A situation only the initiated are likely to understand.

The result is that many farmers tend to remain in the same locality all their lives, held by their allegiance to the land which provides their living. Sometimes it runs to two or three generations, with the farm becoming the senior member of the family. And many a wife has discovered that she has entered into a form of bigamy, finding she is married both to the farmer and to the farm.

I must confess that I am one who committed his life to some 300 East Anglian acres, at first with the foolish belief that eventually, despite the vagaries of weather and climate, control could be imposed. The realisation that this can never be and that nature will always in some way make it a battleground only really comes with age. The true farmer's spirit is such that he is ever the optimist: next year cannot be as bad as the past. Only the optimist stays the course; the realists soon quit and turn to less demanding occupations.

The agricultural hostilities that hold a farmer to his patch of land will, if he stays the pace, eventually see him as one of the father figures of his village. This he may not aspire to, but the continual attrition of other souls may place him there, particularly so today when those whose livelihood is outside agriculture are generally residents for only comparatively brief periods. My long presence in what I can now justifiably call my village has resulted in a consciousness that does not usually befall the itinerant. Not so much the many influences of modern society that have elevated or depressed, depending on one's viewpoint, the community from rural isolation to urban executives' dormitory, but rather the departure, primarily to the churchyard, of those villagers who always seemed to have a certain permanency in one's younger years.

A mental review of the dwellings in the village street and along the lanes reveals that only here and there is a house still occupied by the same folk that were present when I was a lad. It is also a reminder that I am a member of this dwindling few and heading towards the top of the heap!

Happily there are still a few "owd boys and owd girls" who have been around far longer than I have and still retain, through their memories, what I like to think is the true essence of village life. These are the survivors of the days when the roadside verges outside dwellings were rank with wild flowers and not mown lawn-clean and set with white markers; before the lanes were name-signed like town streets; when footpaths were short cuts to the shop or workplace and not dogs' exercise and excreting strips; when pubs sold real ale and nothing more solid to eat than a packet of crisps; when there wasn't a public loo and a boutique in the village street; and when one could venture out on a cycle without the risk of being brushed into the ditch by commuter traffic. Now in the minority, these remnants of the old village families are given to indulging in nostalgia, often heavily embroidered, and to airing memories of bygone days, to seeking out each other and reminiscing about him or her and this or that of years long ago.

Without any doubt the most vociferous exponent of biographical gossip is Old Newson, who was born when Edward VII was on the throne and is still going strong. While there is always a fair element of truth in his yarns, one suspects that his imagination intervenes, particularly when it concerns the finer details which he could not have been privy to, and which those persons involved would be hardly likely to have divulged.

Harry Newson has been drawing a pension for two decades, and even before that I cannot recall him devoting himself with much energy to any particular task. He had a variety of helper jobs around the district, but after inheriting the family smallholding he appears to have taken to semi-retirement and to directing most of his energies to mardling (Suffolk for passing the time of day with chitchat). I feel that the older he gets the more bizarre his tales become.

Old Rue is of similar vintage and worked on this farm regularly for 40 years, and for another 15 part-time after he retired. A regular drinking man, he has long been renowned for the exaggeration of happenings recounted in the local pubs, and which have earned him a good many free pints of mild and bitter over the years. His tales are short and pithy; not monologues like Newson's. Rue always had a very healthy interest in reproductory matters, and his comments on the subject tended to be exceedingly earthy, if not downright coarse. As is common with like individuals, he was labelled a dirty old man by women who had encountered his uncouth narrations, particularly those ageing women who had lost interest in carnal pursuits.

It would not be fair to condemn him, for most farm men were equally as frank, if more guarded. The natural behaviour of the birds, bees and other creatures, particularly humans, was as normal a subject for discussion as might be the season's tomatoes, the parish cricket team, or the declining quality of pale ale.

The other farm men adjudged some of Rue's exploits as wishful thinking, but there were indications that he had been a bit of a lad in his time.

The only other long-term employee on this farm who is still in the district is Archie, one-time horseman and tractor driver. A good dozen years younger than Rue, Archie turned to jobbing gardening in his retirement. In his earlier years he was possessed of an almost tireless energy; it seemed as if he relished hard work. He was not, however, one for gossip, and I do not recall his ever telling an anecdote.

Over the years there were several other employees who stayed for a few years or just a few months; the landgirls, Clive the Welsh cowman, Wernie the ex-prisoner of war, and of course Nasty, who was a rural spiv. These mostly in the days when my father was Guv'nor and the labour force often totalled near a dozen men and women. Since the Guv'nor died the number of employees has gradually diminished as mechanisation increased. Now only Tim and Toby handle all the work, and with comparative ease.

Beyond the farm gate in the village street and along the highways and byways of the parish there existed a wealth of characters, several of whom feature in the following pages. The majority are long gone, and so often my knowledge of their backgrounds is limited. When they were everyday people around the village one's youthful outlook never questioned their mortality. Just as there seemed a permanence about village life, the villagers were part of that permanence. But time was insidiously ticking away at this scene, if only at a rate where if a person died, a new house was built or a tree uprooted, one still assessed the place to be just the same.

Now the effect of this slow erosion is very evident to me. But by the same token, will not those born and bred in the village in the last decade of the twentieth century assume the permanence of their early environment? And will they, in four score and ten years, have similar sentiments to those I now express? I believe they will, but I also doubt that they will be able to look back at characters like those who coloured the days of my early life.

Now many of these long-gone characters seem almost unreal. However, it should be remembered that they were members of a very different society, where physical labour was the norm and life in general much simpler. Communications were poor and travel expensive. The motor car only came within the reach of wage-earning country folk in the middle of the century. Electricity did not reach some rural outposts until that time, and television was a novelty, an "H" aerial on a house being a status symbol. Perhaps the surfeit of sophistication that has descended since drowns out characters, checks the development of eccentricity and individualism. But do I fail to recognise it? Even so, of one thing I am sure, today's generation will never mind the time I knew.

The tales I tell are plucked from a range of half a century and presented in no particular order, but just as they come to mind.

Stinky Smith

THE ONLY objectionable thing about pigs in my book is their smell. Or, to be more precise, the way their smell clings to your clothes and boots after one has been in close proximity. Odourwise a little pig muck goes a very long way, although one is not always aware that the smell still clings. It seems that after considerable exposure to the pong, one's sense of smell is extinguished.

So it was when I happened to be walking out of the farm gate and was confronted with Old Newson and dog out for their afternoon stroll. Old Newson does love a mardle and often hovers near the farm in the hope of cornering an open ear. The problem is that I don't always have the time to listen. On this occasion we had hardly exchanged salutations before he was twitching his nose. 'You bin in them pig sheds ain't yer?', and without waiting for my confirmation, continued, 'You proper hum. You'd best be a'washin' your boots and gettin' out of them overalls before you go in the house. Otherwise your missus is gonner give you a bit of tongue.'

'Is it that bad?' I queried, sniffing my sleeve.

'Well I wouldn't want to cuddle up to yer!' was the rebuke.

'There's only one thing worse than pigs and thas an old billy goat,' continued the sage. I noticed his bull terrier had sat down in expectation of a lengthy interlude in its exercise.

'What about ferrets? They're pretty bad,' I suggested.

'No, ferrets you get used to, and a nanny goat ain't as bad as a ferret, but an old billy goat, never. Thas a killin' smell – 'course, tha's not to an old nanny goat. To them tha's a beautiful stink – like odour Cologne be to us. A whiff of old billy and tha's put a nanny in the mood quick as lightnin'. Every creature have a smell what's horrible to all the others 'cept them of its own kind. Tha's how nature stop one kind from breedin' with another yer know. Just yer think about it; there'd be a right old mix-up otherwise, wouldn't there?'

I felt it would be wise not to question his logic and only muttered an 'Hmmm' in acknowledgement of this revelation.

'Don't know anybody round these parts that has a billy now.' For a moment or two old Newson was deep in thought, and then he continued, 'Yes, last I knew of was the one Smith had.'

'Smith?' I queried, 'Comey Smith or Briar Smith?'

'Neither. Him they called Stinky Smith 'cause of the billy – had that smallholding on the Bergholt road. Don't know who've got the place now, there's been so many changes.'

'No, I don't think I knew that one,' I responded, although I did have a vague recollection of someone keeping goats over there many years back.

'Tha's understandable. There's for ever of Smiths about. You know why don't yer? Tha's cause they all descended from blackies.'

'Blackies?' Surely he wasn't suggesting all Smiths had a negro background?

'Blacksmiths. Tha's 'cause they work by a hot forge all day. There's nothin' like a bit of heat to make yer fertile. Tha's why there's so many Smiths around. Well-known fact that a bit of heat does the trick. I mind when your Wully and his missus wanted to start a family and nothin' happened. I told him he needed a bit of heat, so the next thing I hear is he's lit a damned great bonfire in his garden and has his old gal sticking her backside up against it. Didn't do no good, silly beggar. That were him who needed hottin' up.'

While old Newson indulged in a few chuckles I took the opportunity to divert his discourse back to the original topic. Not that I was particularly interested in goats, but it seemed preferable to instruction on local fertility rites.

'What about this Smith with the billy goat?'

'Oh yes, I was a'comin' to that. Well, he used to do quite a good trade takin' this old billy around to stud. He didn't mind the smell 'cause he'd been with it so long he didn't notice it. Fact he come to smell nearly as high himself. Never changed his clothes I don't wonder – well, bein' an old bachelor, you know how they gets.

'Anyways, you'd often smell him and the billy comin' along the road a while afore they gets to you. When he were takin' it to stud he had it on a long length of light chain, so as when he stopped to light up a fag the billy could get a good feed off the verges and banks. The landlords always made him drink outside the pubs – you can't blame them, they'd lose trade, and besides the beer would get tainted, if they had him in.

'Now I reckon he didn't shave or wash deliberately. He were no fool, and he must have cottoned on that as people didn't like to come near him that could keep him out of a lot of trouble. Boy, he really did pong I'm tellin' yer. Anyways, one hot summer afternoon he and the billy were goin' along the road to Bergholt when a boy from the village come up behind on his motorbike. The young bugger thinks to himself he'll play a prank on Stinky, and as he drives past he cuts the ignition, or whatever they do, and makes the bike backfire. Bang! bang! that go and frighten the billy so much that it bolted in panic. Course, that couldn't get far 'cause tha's on the end of a chain, so that start runnin' the only way it can, round in circles, with Stinky in the middle hanging on and a'cussin'. Only as the billy goes round tha's winding Stinky up with the chain – honest – 'til in the end they both wound up together and toppled over in the road.

'The old billy is a kickin' and Stinky is a hollerin' and trying to undo the catch on its collar. Ain't long before they both roll into the ditch. Well, Stinky finally gets the catch undone and the billy is up and gone like a bullet tha's so frightened. Stinky's bruised and winded and covered with mud and goat crap. When he manages to crawl out of the ditch he's so exhausted he lays on the verge a while. Some gent comes along in a car, stops and starts to get out, but when he gets a whiff he drives off to the nearest phone box and phones the police. "There's a rottin' corpse on the side of the road" he says. Yes, tha's what he told them. When the local bobby come to investigate Stinky is up and searchin' for the billy. "You ought to be arrested for causing a public nuisance or something" says the Bobby. "But even if I knew what to charge you with I'm damned if I'd want the job of taking you into custody".

There was another short interlude for mirth. The red spotted handkerchief was brought out of a coat pocket, and after a couple of dabs at his lips old Newson launched off again. 'Now, as for the billy, that ran a fair way before that calmed down. Nervous things goats. Anyways, tha's luck had changed, for that managed to find its way into the kitchen garden of that big house on the hill just up the road from the King's Head. At that time there was some busybody do-good woman lives there – can't remember her name, double-barrelled Mrs something-or-other. Anyways, she'd got a tea party on her lawn with a half dozen other hoity-toity old gals. Well, they's a'sittin' there nibblin' and sippin' when they gets a whiff of billy. Only being gentry they don't know what it is; no, they sit there

makin' polite conversation and sippin' tea and thinkin' it must be one of themselves tha's got a tummy upset. But nobody says nothin'. There's your gentry for yer. If they had been old country gals one of them would soon have up and say, "Who's dropped a crafty one then?" Weren't long before the gentry women was making excuses and goin' home, and I expect that Mrs double-barrelled something was pleased to see the back of 'em, thinking one old gal must have forgot herself. Anyways, the smell didn't go away, so the missus whatever she were called start looking around and spots the billy fast asleep in the middle of her shrubbery. When she's seen the mess that made in her kitchen garden the old dear nearly go crackers. She phone for the police, the fire brigade, the RSPCA, St John's Ambulance, the vicar and just about everyone you can think of. But none of them would try and catch the goat because that wham so much. The local copper had to go and get Stinky. The woman was for suing Stinky for damages, but the law told her she was wasting her time; no judge and jury would sit in the same court as Stinky.'

'If he was that bad it can't have been very pleasant for his neighbours,' I proffered.

'You're right there,' continued old Newson, 'Bloke who lived on the next smallholding didn't half suffer when the wind were in the west. He used to build his hay and corn stacks along the boundary to block out some of the stink. That artful Stinky; you know what he did? He used to tether his old billy close to the boundary on his side, right behind the stack, so as the goat could get a free feed of hay by stretching its head through the barbed wire fence. Course, the neighbour couldn't see the far side of his stack were being eaten away. But Stinky came unstuck in the end, he were a bit too clever. That billy kept munchin' away until that had made a great hole in the bottom side of that stack. Course, that were undermining the stack so that were top heavy and one day that suddenly toppled over on to Stinky's land while the billy was a'munchin'. Suffocated it, of course. Do you know, Stinky even threatened to prosecute his neighbour for keeping an unsafe stack, but that were only a threat.'

'Did Smith get another billy goat?' I enquired, foolishly.

'No, not a hope. Stinky smelt so high of that billy what got smothered no other billy would have ever took to him. One billy can't abide another, tha's nature again. No, I don't know of anyone who keep a billy round here now. Mind you, if you're a'wantin' to make a bit of pocket money you could do worse than keep a billy, only I won't be comin' to visit yer.'

We both laughed. But I was sorely tempted.

The Great Fog

THERE IS a belief, especially among North Americans, that England is a place frequently beset with fog. Undoubtedly a hangover from the pre-smokeless zone days of big city smog, this vision of foggy England is quite mistaken now fog is rarely more than a heavy mist and nowhere as restrictive as in the past.

Indeed, there has not been a real cloaking fog in these parts since the late 'forties, if my memory serves me correctly; not since what came to be known on this farm as the Great Fog. It featured a period of winter high pressure weather with not a breath of wind for the best part of a week, and we appeared to be set in a permanent high-stacked cloud that grew so thick on a couple of days that at times an object ten yards ahead was lost from view. Those vehicles that ventured out on the roads crept around in first and second gear, which did not prevent the odd one from ending up in a ditch.

I recall it gave Nasty an excuse not to come to work. 'I was afeared of getting run down by a lorry or somethin',' he explained, and when that didn't satisfy the Guv'nor he added that 'The owd dag properly get on my chest if I start breathin' that in.' Rue used the restricted visibility as an excuse, accidentally he says, to grope the landlady of The Anchor on the taproom doorstep. She was not for groping under any circumstances, as Rue's bruised and blackened left eye bore witness. But the Great Fog is probably best remembered on this farm for the humbling of Wully.

Wully had once been cowman, but eventually spurned that task in favour of general farm work. He gravitated to second horseman, which mostly involved carting jobs with the horse and tumbrel. Nobody really relished working with Wully because he was given to tetchiness. He saw no merit in work. Nothing achieved on the farm brought him satisfaction, his apparent attitude to all jobs being that they were an affliction that had to be borne in the cause of obtaining a wage.

It is probable that his irritability stemmed from the discomfort of having fallen arches and walking flat-footed. Wully never walked anywhere further than he could help, and if he had to step out in the course of some task, then best keep out of his way. There probably wasn't a coarser tongue in the district, and he did not hesitate to demonstrate this at the slightest provocation. His impatience was often the trigger, and while landgirls and strangers might be spared the invective, he would still be decidedly acid.

Occasionally he overstepped the mark, notably when a 12-year-old public schoolboy plied him with questions about agricultural practice. Having endured this simple inquisitiveness for some minutes, Wully turned the tables by berating the boy, 'Does your father still get his oats from your mother?' The boy was obviously an innocent for, on returning home, he naively put the question to his parents. The poor old Guv'nor had to suffer a telephoned complaint from an enraged father.

While Wully was not very sociable, he was pretty bright. There were not many dodges he didn't know, and if there was a foul-up on the farm you could be sure it was never Wully's fault. He was acknowledged by all as the supreme crafty old devil. We all wished to get one over him, but Wully was too wily – except on that one occasion during the Big Fog.

On the second day of this enveloping veil the Guv'nor wanted Wully to collect a load of mangles from the clamp to bring into the farmyard for the cattle. The problem was the lack of visibility on the road, and the Guv'nor suggested to Wully that it would be safer to go across the fields. Wully agreed.

The tumbrel had been left at the mangle clamp, and to reach that location it was necessary for Wully to take the horse out of the yard, cross the Home Meadow to the entrance into the Thirty Acre, over that to the gate on the far side and then into the Wood Field where the clamp was situated. A longer journey than by road but undoubtedly safer in the current conditions. So off Wully went, riding sidesaddle on the Suffolk mare. As I have said, Wully never walked anywhere if he could help it.

I had been given the task of mucking out calf pens with Rue, which was not a bad job for such a raw day. Around 10 o'clock the Guv'nor stuck his head in the door and asked if Wully was back with the mangles. We hadn't heard or seen him. The Guv'nor departed, but about five minutes later he was back. 'You'd better go and see what's happened to him, he's been gone nearly an hour. He ought to be back by now.' The directions were to me.

I climbed the yard gate into the Home Meadow and took what I thought was the correct bearing on the gateway into the Thirty Acres. The hoof prints of the horse showed in the mud, but I lost them once I moved further into Home Meadow. Munching cows appeared and disappeared as I progressed through the murk. Home Meadow is only about three acres and it did not take long before I was confronted with the opposite hedge. The immediate problem was whether to turn left or right to find the gateway.

Left seemed the more likely, and I started to follow along the hedge. However, after ten or so yards a familiar holly bush loomed in the hedgerow and I knew that I must be going in the wrong direction. Retracing my footsteps, I continued on and eventually found the gate. Everything was dripping wet, my wool sweater included.

The Thirty Acres was the largest field on the farm and currently down to clover ley. Again I took what I thought was a straight line and set off into the gloom. After a few minutes I stopped and listened. All was silence. It made me feel rather lonely and isolated, although the farm and some houses were only a few hundred yards away. I pressed on at a brisk pace, and the bank and low hedge on the Wood Field boundary finally appeared. Fortunately I recognised an old elm stump on the bank and realised that I was perhaps 300 yards from my goal, the gateway.

Tracking along the ghostly hedgerow I finally came to the gate, which had been left open as there were no cattle on the Thirty Acres. There were plenty of horse hoof marks in the gateway but none looked particularly fresh to me. At the mangle clamp the tumbrel stood forlorn. An examination showed that no one had pounded the ground around the clamp that morning. Now foreboding thoughts sprang to mind: had Wully fallen off the horse? Was he lying injured somewhere? I may not have been particularly keen on the cantankerous old so-and-so, but I didn't wish him harm.

Going back into the Thirty Acres, I decided to return to the farm and get help. As I went I called, 'Wully!', stopping and listening. There was no response. Back at the farm, I expressed my fears. With the Guv'nor, Rue, Wernie and Clive in tow I returned to the Thirty Acre. 'Spread out and keep calling' was the Guv'nor's brief, and off we set. Within a couple of minutes I had twice bumped into Rue. 'Stop buggering about boy, we ain't playin' kiss-in-the-ring' was his admonition. I groped on, sense of direction flown in the oppressive mists. Then I thought I heard the clink of chain. Stopping to listen, I heard it again. 'Wully,' I roared. There was no answering call but the clink of chain grew closer. Then out of the gloom, in almost frightening bulk, loomed the mare with Wully astride its back. 'Wully,' I yelled, 'where have you been?'

'Blast boy, you'll frighten the bloody hoss,' he scolded; but his voice lacked the usual venom.

'We're all searching for you. We thought you'd fallen off,' I explained excitedly.

'Tha's this fog, I must have bin miles.' There was a definite note of concern in his voice, and he hadn't even countered my suggestion that he, of all people, might fall off a horse.

'What do you mean, miles? You're still in the Thirty Acres,' I queried.

'I was just a'comin' back,' was his sheepish explanation.

'But you must have known which field you were in when you went through the gateways,' I pressed the point.

'Couldn't see 'em. The fog's so thick,' he replied; even more unconvincingly.

'It's not that thick. I could see the gateways plain enough when I went through.'

'Well, that must have bin thicker a while back 'cause I couldn't see 'em. Couldn't hardly see the hoss, that were so thick in some places.'

It was obviously pointless to argue. Wully was going to stick to his story, but I was pretty sure he hadn't been out of the Thirty Acres for whatever reason.

It took some time to extract everybody else from the Thirty Acre fog, all decidedly damp and not very happy with Wully. Everyone ridiculed his account of having been miles, persist as he might. Not until the end of the week when a breeze blew up and the vapours disappeared did the truth emerge. Walking across the Thirty Acre I could see hoof prints, and as I followed them they continually veered gently left until completing a wide circle. Obviously Wully, riding on the horse, had been taking what he thought was a straight line across the field towards the gate, but the mare had just been going round in circles all the time! Wully would not have it when this was pointed out to him, insisting he had been miles; he had, only all in the same field! Still, it gave Rue, Clive and the others the ammunition they had long wanted to deride Wully.

On reflection, I think Wully sounded quite relieved when I appeared through the fog. The puzzle is, why didn't he hear us calling? Perhaps the fog muffled the sound, and in such a large field he might not have heard. On the other hand, and more likely, perhaps he did hear and didn't like to answer, hoping he could eventually find his own way out.

He was never allowed to forget the incident. For years after, whenever there was the slightest hint of fog, the men would suggest to Wully that it was a good day for riding rings on the Thirty Acres. Wully ignored the taunts. However, he came to develop his own story line, and regaled strangers encountered in The Anchor's snug with how he'd ridden halfway to Ipswich and back in the Great Fog. Of course, not when any of us were present.

Mud

AH, THE impetuosity of youth. What it is to know better than your elders, and to be eager to prove that you do. Only the passing years bring sobriety and the acknowledgement that the older generation was right after all. But youth does not have that perception, and in asserting its beliefs frequently comes unstuck. Although in the sorry tale I recount to illustrate the proposition, unstuck was the antithesis of the situation.

We had suffered a particularly dry summer and the pastures had more shades of brown than green. The milking herd was being fed hay and added concentrates to make up for the dearth of grass. Like humans who are forced to a restricted diet and have a craving for those eats and drinks that are taboo, so cattle lust for lush grass or more succulent greenery in times of drought. They will stand and look longingly at the sugar beet in the next field, even more so at the brassicae in somebody's kitchen garden. And should there be a weakness in the fence or hedge, the temptation will prove too much.

It was breakfast time when Clive the cowman banged on the kitchen door, opened it and informed the Guv'nor, 'Hazel is in the pond. She won't come out.'

'Okay, I'll get some help.' The Guv'nor looked at me. Why was it always me who had to sacrifice the satisfaction of his cornflakes whenever there was a mealtime emergency?

'All right, I'll go,' I said grudgingly as the Guv'nor again disappeared from view behind his Daily Mail.

When I arrived in the collecting meadow there were already three spectators, Wully, Rue and Archie, who must also have been informed by Clive of the errant cow. The pond, roughly rectangular in shape, was in the corner of the field. The sides in the field corner were backed by a thick, overgrown hedge beyond which was a deep ditch and the road. Nothing short of a bulldozer could reach the pond from that side.

The pond was reasonably shallow, and its waters often receded in times of drought. On this particular occasion scorching sun and no rain for weeks had reduced the water to no more than two or three small pools on the far side. But for a small spring that continually fed the pond at one end, it would have dried out completely. In one of these small pools Hazel, the Friesian, reposed. It was easy to see what had attracted her to drag belly and bag through the mud; an abundance of green herbage that clothed patches of the bank below the hedge where its brambles did not crowd out on to the pond. The cow stood munching and dolefully viewing the audience.

'I've tried shouting and calling,' said Wully, 'the bugger won't come out.'

'You won't budge her 'til she's done her eatin',' observed Rue, dryly.

'I wouldn't wonder if she's stuck. Might have to get a tractor to pull her out,' was Archie's contribution.

'What about throwing something at her,' was my bright suggestion, and I moved off to the end of the pond, picked up a rotten branch from the bottom of the hedge and broke it in half. My first throw splashed down beside Hazel and might have raised no more than a flinch. The second was more accurate and landed on her rump. All this produced was a shudder.

'You'll just make things worse if you keep doing that,' scolded Wully.

The Guv'nor had arrived on the scene by then and after a discussion with his stalwarts observed 'We'll just have to leave her until she decides to come out.'

'I can get her out,' I declared, 'if I go and get my Wellingtons on I can wade out there and drive her out.'

'Don't be so daft, boy, you'll get stuck in that lot. You can see that's like treacle,' Rue cautioned.

'No, I've walked in there many a time. If the cow can wade in there I'm sure I can.' As I made off to get my rubber boots I heard Rue say, 'The boy won't listen. You see, he'll get stuck.' But I'd show 'em.

When I returned to the pond everyone else had gone about their work, which was a good thing because if I had to abandon the attempt there would be no one watching to say, 'I told you so' and make other caustic remarks. Hazel was still munching and watched disinterestedly as I took the first tentative steps. No problem; hadn't I sploshed through the mud in this pond many times when a youngster? On one occasion I stood in it and threw a mud ball at Rue while he was trying to mend a grass mower. He did not appreciate the joke and threatened a clip round the ear. As I was only about seven at the time his usual language was somewhat modified.

Yes, I had splodged about in the mud of that pond many times after moorhens' eggs or the bullrushes that grew up at one end. No problem. As each squelching step was taken in my halting progress towards the cow my boots sank deeper into the mud. I began to wonder if, as a 21-year-old, I was at more of a disadvantage than when I played in the mud as a small boy. For another thing, I had never been quite so far out into the pond. About half way and still some yards from Hazel, I decided the mud was going to come over the top of my boots if the enterprise were continued. A rapid turn round and exit and no one would know I had ever attempted to wade in, particularly if I could quickly clean my boots at the spring.

I started to change direction and found my left foot starting to move up the boot while the boot stayed put. The boots were not a tight fit, because one always had a size larger than normal when buying Wellingtons to allow for an extra pair of thick socks to be worn during the winter. By forcing the top of my foot against the boot I managed, at last, to get the boot free and take another step. The lapse of time was such that my right boot just would not move, and the mud was coming perilously close to the top. I tried moving the left boot again, but that was now equally anchored. I was stuck.

Really stuck!

Although never a panicky type, it was not difficult to think of one of those movie scenes where the villain sinks slowly into an all-consuming quicksand. I could shout for help, but it was doubtful if anyone would have heard above the noise of a popping John Deere tractor that had been started up in the yard. The real bar against shouting for help was the ridicule that would subsequently have to be endured. The only alternative was to roll up my trousers and pull each leg from its boot, sink my legs barefoot into the mud, pull out each boot by hand and struggle back to land. The decision was made: each foot was drawn free, a highly difficult feat if I were not to topple over, which I very nearly did.

Eventually both feet were sunk into the ooze and I sank almost up to my knees. Retrieve the boots I could not. The suction was so great it proved impossible to wrench them free, try as I might. They were already filling with mud, and as I was convinced I too was all the

time sinking further into the mire, I decided to abandon the boots and make for the hard.

It was not easy, and several times I all but sat down or pitched forward. Eventually I made it, my legs and hands caked, my trousers and shirt bespattered. The darned stuff was everywhere, even bits in my hair. I prayed no one would come back into the field until I had time to get to the spring and get some of the mess washed off.

At that moment there was a movement behind me and I turned to see that darned cow slip-slopping its way across the pond as if there were no great problem in shifting one hoof after another. I am not usually given to using invective, but I did about that cow. It made me feel better, and better still on realising that the men would think I had driven the beast out of the pond.

Hazel made off in the direction of the cowshed and I attempted to clean myself up. By watching to see who was about, it proved possible to stagger barefoot across the yard to the house without being seen. Only I was not allowed in the house in that condition and had to use the outside tap. Even with a change of clothes the stench of the mud clung, and I was not popular either inside or outside the house. But I was able to boast, untruthfully, that my efforts had got the cow out of the mud.

There was the matter of a good pair of Wellington boots. That evening a reconnaissance revealed that their exact location was already in doubt as all the footprints, hardly the right description, in the centre of the pond had disappeared. I dreamed up various schemes for trying to extract them over the following days, none really satisfactory. Then the drought broke and within a few weeks the pond had filled again. I gave them up as lost and a new pair had to be purchased, an expensive exercise on the meagre wage I was getting in those days. The Guv'nor's wife soon spotted that her son had new Wellingtons standing in the back door perch and wanted to know why. I felt I could truly say I thought the old ones had been stolen.

We have had other severe droughts in more recent years and, if I remember, I always take a look at the pond to see if a pair of wellies have surfaced, but there is never a sign of them. In the future, millions of years hence, some superior beings will discover them, fossilised, and rave about the find much as is done with dinosaurs today. Who knows, they may end up in what will then pass for a museum. And will they identify them as the cast footwear of the species Rogerious Freemansaurus?

The Marrying Kind

FOR SOME reason Tim's tractor refused to start. Air getting into the diesel system was the diagnosis, and I was trying to find out how.

'You got trouble?' I looked up to see the familiar weathered face beaming at me.

'Think so,' I responded.

He edged in the partly opened workshop door, seated himself on the tractor's front tyre and leaned forward on his stick; the usual signs that there was some hot gossip to impart. 'Hear about Owd Margie?'

'Margie?' I queried; and then I remembered a somewhat notorious old baggage who was the cause of a lot of speculation a few years back. 'What Margie er...? The one who was once married to the old boy who lived in that thatched house on the Ipswich Road at Bergholt?'

'Yes, tha's her. She's just got herself wed again.'

'Heavens,' I exclaimed, 'she must be getting a bit long in the tooth. Surprised to hear she's still around.'

'Let me see,' he mused, 'she'd be...75...no, 76.' Then, after an involved account of how he arrived at this precise figure, he paused, to achieve maximum impact, and triumphantly announced, 'It's her sixth!'

'What, sixth marriage! Good grief.' Even I was a little taken aback. In rural East Anglia three times married for folk is rare; six times must be a record. 'Getting as bad as America,' was my added thought.

'Well, she's the marryin' kind, ain't she.' Despite my failure to ask why, old Newson was off. No stopping him now. I readied my 'Umms' and 'Well I nevers'.

'This owd boy she's just wedded is 85 and they tell me he's got a wooden leg and a tube, so don't sound as if he'll be consecratin' the marriage.'

I should have let him continue, but not really thinking I queried, 'A tube?'

'Surely you knows about the length of plastic tube they shove up yer when your prostrate get furred up? Had it done to me about four years ago. Christmas Eve it were. Probably been knockin' back too much of me owd mushroom wine – that properly stir the owd worms up for yer – anyways, I found I couldn't make water so the doc packed me off to emergency at the hospital. Real 'barrassing that were. A couple of nurses had me flat out on a table and me breeches off afore you could say Father Christmas. They was poundin' my weddin' tackle about like the butcher stringing up a pound of pork sausages. I say to 'em, "Go easy now. Times was when I wouldn't have minded a couple of young women like you a handlin' me" but before I could say more one of 'em shut me up real proper.

'"Tha's enough out of you Mr Newson" she snap, "any more clever remarks like that and we'll tie a knot in it and shove a piece of mistletoe up the end." Did ever you hear the likes of that?'

'Could have been worse,' I quickly interjected, 'they might have threatened holly. But what about this old fellow Margie married?' I wanted to avoid being given a detailed description of old Newson's urinary problems.

'Oh yes, as I was sayin', I doubt he'll be long for this world. 'Course, you can bet the owd fellow hev got a pound or two put by. Tha's always been her game, ain't it? No flies on her, boy. She come from a hard-working family too. Her two sisters were dab hands at beet bashin' and spud pickin', but Margie wouldn't do nothin' like that if she could help it. Pretty gal, and when she found out what tickled men's fancies she didn't take long in workin' out how she could put it to advantage. When she were about 18 – that'd be around '34 – got that great oaf what have Dell Farm to marry her by makin' out she was expectin'. 'Course, he was as damp as a duckpond, otherwise he'd ha' known that was a put-up job. After she'd got the ring and he asked her why she weren't beginnin' to show she told him she's said she was expectin' to, not goin' to. Weren't long afore she was properly rulin' the roost. Kept that feller on the hop. Wouldn't let him drink and he a drinkin' man. Know how he got round it? He got a young lad to fill up veterinary bottles with whisky and label them as horse dose. Kept it in the stable and whenever he wanted a nip he'd nip out and pretend he'd gone to dose the horse. 'Course, the darned fool got the bottles mixed up. You can guess what he done can't you?'

'He drank the true horse dose,' I ventured.

'No, no. Forced a quart of neat scotch down the neck of a great owd cob 'cause that looked a bit off colour. Well, as you'd expect, that owd horse went out like a light; collapses right on top of him. Suffocated he were. They tried artificial restitution on him but that were no good.'

'Respiration,' I corrected.

'Tha's what I said.' There was annoyance in his voice, so I struck a sympathetic note.

'How terrible for Margie.'

'Her! She weren't worried. Reckoned she'd have sold both him and the horse to the knackers if she could have done. He was only a tenant, so when things were sold up she didn't get much. Farmers weren't rollin' in money like you together are nowadays. Never mind, Margie weren't six months findin' another husband. As I told yer, she were the marryin' kind.'

And seeing my quizzical look he elaborated, 'Tha's men that usually pops the question and does the marryin', ain't it? Women ain't all that keen, you know; you can't blame 'em not wantin' to spend their lives a'cookin' for old boys, scrubbing floors and wipin' kids snotty noses. No, if it weren't for the matin' feelin' most of 'em wouldn't get wed. You can't blame 'em. Yes, tha's the matin' feelin' that gets 'em. Anyways, there's some women, like owd Margie, what does the marryin'. They ain't much interested in men; tha's their goods and chattels they're after. 'Course, tha's common enough with the gentry women and them film stars nowadays, the peapers is always full of their marryin' goin's on.'

'Mercenary,' I commented.

'No, they don't show much mercy once they get their hands on a man, least not Margie. As I said, she weren't long lookin' around for another, and she set her sights on the undertaker at Wenham. He hadn't long been widowed but he were more than twice Margie's age – about 65 if I remember rightly – and as thin and as pasty looking so as you'd think he was death warmed up. I reckon Margie knew he wouldn't be long before he'd be usin' his own handiwork. What she did to get in there was when her first husband popped off she didn't go to Charlie Gaybarrow for a cheap job like most in this village would, but gets on her bike and cycles all the way to Wenham to see this undertaker. 'Course, she'd got one of them ulterior motions. Weren't long before she were takin' that fellow apple pies and helpin' out in his house. As you can guess, that weren't long either before she was slippin' between the sheets and raisin' his temperature, and then there's no fool like a man. The next thing we hears he's been churched. But she'd made a mistake; his undertakin' business were hardly payin' its way; long-livin' lot at Wenham, and he charged too much. Besides, they could get a better deal at the Co-op what paid a divi' in them days; made you feel better if you knew you were going to get a bit of money back on whoever you was buryin'. Anyways, Margie she didn't half give that little fellow a hard time once she found out how things were goin'. Tried her best to buck him up, but he weren't up to it. Don't think they'd been married a year afore I heard he was a gonner. Some say as how he died on the nest. Tha's been the downfall of a lot of old fellows what forgets their appetite don't get old with 'em.'

As there was a longer than usual pause I looked up from my tussle with the diesel system and saw that old Newson was lighting one of his home-rolled cigarettes. After a few draws and a few puffs, the saga of Margie was continued.

'She struck a bit luckier with her third. He was the randy young doctor what had seen to him she'd just buried. Only they were after different things. A doctor ain't allowed to carry on with a patient so that were wedding bells again.'

During the pause for another draw on his fag I asked, 'What became of him?'

'Little owd Hitler did the job.'

'Oh, he was killed in the war?'

'No, not him. He volunteered, and the next thing we heard he'd run off with one of them little air force waifs.'

'Don't you mean a Waaf?' I suggested.

'Perhaps I do. Anyways, Margie got a fair whack of money out of the divorce settlement, and having been married to a doctor she'd gone up in the world, so to speak. Took on fancy ways like womenfolk do when they get a bit of money, you know, sippin' sherry instead of knockin' back a half of stout. Took her time findin' another fellow. Got a bit choosy. She weren't goin' back to guttin' rabbits and emptying the bucket like a good countrywoman used to take in her stride; Margie were for stickin' with cucumber sandwiches and the flush. Well, there weren't all that many well-to-do fellows around after the war. She tried her stuff on a retired army major, a bachelor who ran the Boy Scout troop at Longham. Turns out to be a waste of time 'cause he was more interested in boy scouts than her. Finally she landed a secondhand car dealer, but that were a job. Bound to be when the fellow had spent his life havin' trade-ins and things on the never-never. He weren't a'goin' to make an outright purchase, was he? Anyway, she finally got a ring out of him and then changes her tune and sets about makin' his life hell. Playin' for the old divorce goal she were. This bloke stuck it for a few years, but he finally made a run for it. Reckon she thought she'd come out of that one with a Rolls-Royce, but she didn't get enough out of the Court to buy a Mini.'

There was another pause for extinguishing and discarding the cigarette butt. Finding I could not concentrate on my tractor problem and listen to this gripping saga at the same time, I sat down on the other tractor front wheel, 'That makes four. What about the fifth?'

'Wait you on, I was just a'comin' to that. After number four I reckon she thought tha's easier to deal with the owd fellows than divorce the young uns. And she weren't as young as she was either. Still, her luck was in 'cause she got to know an owd fellow who was

in amusements – reckon he were about 70. Mind you, Margie was puttin' on the years by then; well in her fifties. Anyways, he had a lot of these fruity machines at the seaside places up and down the coast, Clacton, Southend, Yarmouth and the likes. I ain't ever seen one of these fruity machines but they tell me you puts in a few pennies and all these fruits whirl around like catherine wheels. If when they stops there's three lemons in a little window the machine coughs up a few quid. Sounds daft to me.'

'One-armed bandit,' was my helpful comment, but old Newson looked a bit puzzled.

'He were a bloody crook all right, but I never heard that he only had one arm.'

I would have explained if there had been a chance to get a word in edgeways. The raconteur was again in full stride.

'That were all cash, and you can be sure the owd income tax boys didn't get their hands on much of it. Why, Margie couldn't have done better, 'cause that had all to be spent on the quiet and she knew how to spend all right! Just like an owd sow that's broke into a full meal shed she were. Always a'drivin' around in new cars, a darned great Jaguar mostly. And you should have seen her, done up like a dog's dinner with fur coats and drippin' with jewellery. Didn't recognise her when I first saw her with that owd fellow, she'd gone bromide blonde.'

'I think you mean peroxide,' I dared to correct.

'Well, happen I do, makes no difference, she looked proper disgustin' for a woman her age. All right for the gentry women to doll themselves up so they look like fairground aunt sallies, but you'd think a woman from good country stock would know better. Anyways, Margie was all for keepin' this owd fellow a'goin' strong. This was one she wanted to hang on to. He were like the goose what laid the golden eggs. She kept him goin' for several years but as I told you, he were about 70 when they married. Darned if one day one of them fruity machines went wrong, reckon the fruit were goin' off or somethin' as they kept comin' up three lemons each time and paid out hundreds of pounds. The shock of losing all that cash was too much for the owd fellow and his owd ticker gave out there and then.'

'Rough luck on Margie, but surely he left her nicely off?'

'Reckon she had a few quid and the house and the car, but you're forgettin' that were all cash. Sooner spent. Never mind, she should be all right this time.'

At this point I managed to insert an 'Oh?'

'Yes. I hear the new hubby was once an insurance sales manager, and they fellows always had to have a bit of their own, so to speak. You can be sure he'll have some nice fat pension policies.'

'Sounds as if she won't have to bother with a seventh when this one goes then,' I speculated.

'Don't you be so sure. Didn't I tell you she was the marryin' kind? They don't change their ways, not they. Well, I mustn't sit here a'listenin' to you. Left my little owd dog at home and he'll need his afternoon feed.'

With that the sage slowly raised himself from his wheel seat and began to make for the door. For once I saw an opportunity to tease and called after him, 'I reckon you'd suit Margie down to the ground if ever she needs a seventh.' Old Newson turned, a mischievous grin on his face. 'She'd soon be put off seein' me queuing for me pension. 'Sides, a fellow can't marry his sister!'

And with that he was gone. I should have known better, one never really gets the last word with Harry Newson.

Poodle

OBSTINACY is a familiar characteristic of older generations of countrymen. Perhaps this is a facet of the spirit of independence that thrived in the earlier part of this century despite the "master and man" situation in society. I recall some stubborn old codgers around here, and without doubt there was none more so than Poodle.

In many respects Poodle remained something of a mystery; notably that no one in the village now knows where he came from or where he went. Even old Newson, the venerable sage who is a mine of information on parishioners past and present, is stumped and can do no better than, 'I think he come just afore the war and moved away just about the time there was that scandal about them two women down the council houses both being put in the family way by the postman.' In village history such happenings as the latter take precedence over national events, but from the age of the resulting progeny I gather Poodle moved away in the late 'fifties.

Nor does anyone appear to know what he had previously done for a living, although the speculation is that he had been in the Services and derived a pension. He certainly had no regular employment that I know of while living in this village. His surname was Diggins, but no one seems to know his first name or how he came to be called Poodle. In a small village where it is usual for everyone to know everything about everybody, Poodle's preserved privacy can be traced to his generally uncommunicative nature and his occupancy of a red brick and slate 'thirties-built eyesore that reposes in isolation near the parish boundary. Moreover, wives are usually the chief source of gossip but Mrs Poodle never seemed to venture out from the house. In fact, I do not remember seeing her once and even old Newson, who had a keen eye for the ladies, confesses that he caught sight of her on only a couple of occasions when he called at Poodle's.

Poodle's standing in the community was that of a helping hand. Because he had no regular employment and was usually found at home, he was frequently sought for all manner of tasks where his evident strength would be beneficial. Although a middle-aged man in my memory, I would say he was born around the turn of the century, he was stocky, upright and evidently very fit. Where muscle was needed it was a case of "go and see if Poodle will lend a hand".

He was invariably clad in bib and brace overalls but always clean and tidy. Thinning ginger hair topped a pumpkin-shaped head with small features. I recall the narrow piggish eyes that gave the impression of a permanent frown. And it was in the matter of his eyesight that Poodle's obstinacy ruled supreme. There was little wrong with his long vision but he definitely had problems seeing close by. Despite this deterioration in sight, he refused to get himself spectacles, professing that there was nothing wrong with his vision and that he didn't believe in glasses anyway. The printed word must have been a blur, but he passed this off by declaring that he had never been one for reading.

His failing eyesight became evident when he declined to hit nails with a hammer and would occasionally trip over things while helping out. Then there was the incident when he had been recruited to help erect new goalposts on the sports field. On finishing, Poodle put on his jacket and split a sleeve at the shoulder. This did not please the real owner of the jacket when he found Poodle had picked up the wrong one. The "why don't you get yourself some bloody glasses" rebuke might just as well have fallen on deaf ears. 'I can see what I'm doin' all right. I don't need glasses. Nothin' wrong with my eyesight.'

Then there was the nonsense at the Coronation Gala. Bill Stokes, who ran the village taxi, was in charge of logistics for the pageant and went to see Poodle. 'We'll need a gang of fellows to shift some of the props and scenery at the sports field on the day. There has to be some quick changes. Got to get King Alfred's baking oven out of the way so that Drake's ship can be wheeled on.' Poodle said he didn't mind helping before the event but he wasn't going to come on the day. He didn't like crowds. 'Look, I'll tell you what I'll do. I'll pick you up in my taxi and as soon as the pageant is over and the kids' party starts I'll drive you straight home,' Bill persisted. Poodle was finally persuaded on the condition that Bill would be ready, without fail, to drive him home as soon as the heaving was finished. As a further inducement the taxi would convey Poodle to the rehearsals held during the evenings before the great day, as Bill had also to collect and return a lady involved in the pageant players' wardrobe.

The village Coronation Gala was opened by The Honourable Mrs Something-or-Other from Hadleigh, whose husband once held office in connection with the Privy Purse. Fortunately, the lady was not privy to the ribald comments aired in The Wheelwright's Arms about such an appointment. The pageant was surprisingly good for an amateur production, and the only hiccup was during Queen Elizabeth the First's speech to her troops when a 12-year-old soldier could not resist the temptation and prodded the bottom of a 14-year-old lady-in-waiting standing in front of him. Unfortunately, the girl's agonized exclamation of 'You wait, you rotten little bugger' was picked up by the microphone, thus adding a certain piquancy to the performance.

The pushers and shovers of props completed their task with alacrity and Poodle, who had for once donned a reasonable dark suit in place of the usual bib and brace attire, quite enjoyed himself. The Honorable Mrs Something-or-Other had just been ushered into her chauffeur-driven 1938 Armstrong-Siddeley by the vicar and the chairman of the Parish Council when Poodle strutted out of the sports field, opened the back door of the Armstrong-Siddeley and got in. The assembled village dignitaries were rather taken aback but evidently thought this was by some prior arrangement and that Poodle had previously made the acquaintance of the lady. She, for her part, was even more taken aback when Poodle suddenly appeared on the seat beside her, but concluded he had been delegated as some sort of escort by the parish dignitaries. In any case, she was not given time for enquiry as Poodle commanded, 'Well, get goin' Bill, don't hang about.'

While the chauffeur was also surprised by the newcomer, William being his first name, he immediately obliged. The Armstrong-Siddeley had not rolled out of sight before Bill Stokes' old Wolseley chugged noisily out of the car park into the lane and halted. 'Anyone seen Diggins?' he enquired of the still-puzzled vicar and his entourage. 'He's just gone with the lady,' the vicar responded, gesturing in the direction of the departing Armstrong-Siddeley. 'We thought it rather strange. Do you know if they are acquainted?'

Bill Stokes' reaction was undoubtedly muted because of the company: 'I told him to be in the lane here at 5 o'clock and I'd take him home. I know what he's done. He's got in the wrong car. Darned fool can't see proper. We keep telling him he should get glasses.'

Evidently Poodle was not immediately aware of his error, for after a few moments of silence he addressed his fellow traveller, whom he thought was the village woman who had ridden down beside him to the gala, with the following comment on the vegetable competition: 'Did you see the size of Rue Scrutt's marrow? Course that had been forced under glass. I wouldn't want to eat it, he empty his bucket over it you know.'

Obviously somewhat perplexed, the lady could only mumble a feeble 'Oh,' apparently insufficient for Poodle to realize it was not whom he thought beside him. However, looking ahead he saw that the road taken did not go anywhere near his abode. 'Where you off to Bill? I told you I wanted to go straight home. Must feed my hens afore they think about roosting.' It was then that the chauffeur realised that something was amiss, and through following exchanges Poodle was made embarrassingly aware of his error.

The chauffeur, whose account is the basis of our knowledge of events, said that his employer accepted Poodle's apologies and even diverted from her intended route so that he could be deposited near to his home. Of course, Poodle divulged nothing to his associates and warded off the chaffing from the locals with no more than, 'I knew what I were doing!'

Even this incident failed to demolish Poodle's obstinacy in refusing to obtain a pair of glasses. It has ever since provided a good yarn to relate to Yuppies for those old uns in The Wheelwright's bar seeking a free pint. If that fails to conjure up a round of drinks, Poodle's most famous lapse will almost certainly do the trick. And this episode I can vouch for, having been present myself.

Sometimes during the mid-fifties there was one of those tearing autumn gales that sends leaves and twigs flying, flips the odd roof tile and occasionally topples a weakling tree. The phone rang early Sunday morning. The widowed Mrs McGregor living in the Old Parsonage House had a beech down across her drive. Can I muster help to cut it up? The district nurse comes to administer to Mrs McGregor's invalid sister each day and won't be able to get up the drive. So I picked up Rue and Tim and set off with bow saws and cross-cuts. No whizz-bang chain saws in those days, well, not for the likes of us.

On arrival we found four other helpers already at work, including Poodle. Poodle was in his element on the end of the big cross-cut, but even so it took several hours to log the trunk, all of three feet in diameter at its base. Mrs McGregor showed her gratitude by asking us in for a "fortifier" as she called it. A bottle of malt whisky was produced, among other goodies.

It cannot have been a case of drinking too much, quantitively that is, and more likely a case of prostate gland playing up. For while we all sat in her parlour enjoying the good widow's hospitality, Poodle asked if he could use her toilet in a hurry. 'Down the passage. Door on the left,' I heard her say. Poodle departed and reappeared and I doubt if any of us gave it another thought until Mrs McGregor went to get some sausage rolls she had in the oven. We heard an exclamation of horror coming from the passage, sufficient to check our conversation. Almost immediately Mrs McGregor reappeared in the door. She stood there in a state of shock and could only murmur, 'In my bread bin!' as we assisted her to a chair. Suddenly the penny dropped. I went to have a look. Sure enough there were two doors on the left side of the passage, the first being the pantry, the second the toilet.

'That's a bit dark in there and I didn't know that that was a white enamel bread bin' was Poodle's embarrassed excuse.

'But you took the lid off it before you did it,' I scolded.

'Well, I thought it was one of them old-fashioned "bumbies" that had lids.'

I never saw him wearing them, but I am told that thereafter Poodle did acquire and carry a pair of specs in his pocket. Nevertheless he continued to protest, 'Nothin' wrong with my eyesight.'

Sodding Sykes

IN HIS TIME Major Bobby Sykes would have been appraised as a cad or blighter by the local upper crust with whom he associated. As they tended to keep closed ranks, about the strongest condemnation ever mentioned was that he was a rascal.

His notoriety sprang chiefly from his unbridled use of bad language. He seemed incapable of an utterance that was not embellished by some swear word or obscenity, mostly the adjective sodding. From the frequency of this word's use he became well known in the district as "Sodding Sykes". Presumably the habit of flavouring his speech in this way was a hangover from army days, but even in the late 'forties sodding was still somewhat shocking in nice company. Its use in a BBC radio play would have brought a flood of complaints. However, Sykes did not hesitate to use four-letter obscenities if so minded, often without regard as to who was present. Four-letter words might be heard in the farmyard, but usually only for the descriptive terms they were. Their use as invective was, in those days, chiefly confined to the armed services, dockers and the aristocracy. Elsewhere such utterances were taboo, decidedly criminal.

This did not inhibit Sykes, and while it led to his being ostracised by some of the more sensitive gentry, he was notably popular with a number of middle-aged ladies. Perhaps profanities fascinated when delivered in a strong Oxford accent, but more likely the Major could turn on the charm for these mostly well-off widows and married women whose husbands were frequently absent from home.

There was no doubt that Sodding Sykes revelled in the knowledge that people thought him a womanizer. His favourite transportation around the villages was a fine, docile chestnut mare which was often to be seen tethered to the gate or in the front drive of the house of one of the ladies he was visiting, when it could just as easily have been hidden from view behind the house.

Any reference by his friends to these visits brought a beaming acknowledgement. When questioned on his attraction to 50-year-olds, Sykes' crude response was, 'Don't want any bloody bitches I visit getting in the sodding family way, do I? Ha ha!'

The matrons of his most regular attention were, in most cases, exceedingly plain, and when this too was queried it was met with the hackneyed jibe, 'Who's the silly bugger who wants to look at the sodding mantelpiece when he's pokin' the bloody fire, uh?'

In reality I do not believe that Sodding Sykes was inclined towards amorous adventures. He simply encouraged the reputation as a boost to his ego. A more likely reason for his cultivating friendships with these ladies was the opportunity to empty whisky decanters and perhaps negotiate the odd helpful loan. Sodding Sykes' army pension was probably strained to support the mortgage and rates on the gentleman's country mini-mansion that he had acquired.

While his lifestyle was not unduly lavish, the hue of nose and cheeks surrounding his large military moustache indicated a more than healthy addiction to strong liquor. The empty bottles regularly awaiting the dustman's collection outside his back door appeared to give confirmation. The other pleasure and strain on his finances was riding the chestnut to hounds, rarely missing a local meet, and even indulging in the extravagance of having the horse transported by cattle float to the Waveney Valley and South Essex Hunts.

An indication of his impecuniosity was his inability or disinclination to settle bills. The butcher, baker, grocer and milkman, to name but a few, were regularly engaged in the difficult task of wresting money from Sodding Sykes, who would delay payment as long as possible by plausible excuses and other evasive tactics. When finally payment was made, it was done in person and invariably accompanied by another order, 'Sorry I've taken so sodding long to bring you this cheque. Couldn't find my bloody cheque book. Turned up beside the bog. Wife been using it for bog paper I expect, ha ha! Now, I'd like to take a joint of beef, a couple of dressed chickens and a pound of pork sausages.' The cheque would never actually be handed over until more goods had been received. The Major always seemed to get away with it, probably because the profanity tended to intimidate the shopkeeper, who would not feel comfortable until Sykes was off the premises. Most village tradesmen were wise to Sodding Sykes' manoeuvring, yet they all continued to deal with him.

We farm folk should have been immune to Sodding Sykes' financial jiggery-pokery; we were not. One wet October day the Guv'nor was chatted up by Sodding Sykes in the village street and in a weak moment was persuaded to sell him a load of hay for his horse. The bill accompanied the delivery, but only Mrs Sykes was at home and she promised to get her husband to send a cheque. Of course, nothing came.

Over the following weeks, whenever the Guv'nor chanced to meet the major, verbal requests for payment were met with evasive statements such as, 'Sorry Old Bean, wife's gone off to London with the sodding cheque book.' Or, 'Want to pay you in cash, got the notes in my sodding wallet. Damned if I haven't left the bloody thing in my other jacket.' The excuses were always delivered in a cheerful, almost disarming, manner.

Mrs Sykes was a handy scapegoat on these occasions, although one suspects she was in ignorance of this. An industrious woman, she was often seen bent over in her valiant efforts to bring some order to the large garden surrounding her abode. Sodding Sykes was not for helping; 'If the old girl wants to bugger about with a few bloody hollyhocks, that's up to her, silly bitch.' One suspects she was also in ignorance of the irreverent way in which her husband often referred to her.

One day, just before Christmas, the Guv'nor was walking up the Buttermarket in Ipswich when he spied Sodding Sykes walking towards him on the opposite pavement. Sykes obviously spotted the Guv'nor at the same time and, anticipating a further request for payment of the outstanding account, decided to take the initiative.

The Buttermarket was the select shopping street of the town in those days, and on this occasion was filled with Christmas shoppers, predominantly women. They were, to say the least, taken aback to hear the bellowed salutation, 'Hello Freeman, you old fucker. Bet you're up to no good. Ha ha ha!'

Nowadays, when they are almost obligatory in TV drama, one might not turn a hair at a four-letter obscenity heard in such a public place; then it was almost unthinkable, scandalous. Eyes were first directed at the grinning Sykes and then across the road to whom he was grinning at. The gaze of shocked women rested on the Guv'nor. Having been so addressed in the farmyard he might not have given it a second thought, but in the busiest and most select street in Ipswich it brought instant and acute embarrassment. Everywhere he looked people appeared to be staring at him.

In a state of mental panic he took the first escape route from the scene that he could find, an adjacent shop door. Only when he had shut it firmly behind him did he see where he had entered. All around was lingerie; brassieres, slips and panties; his embarrassment was compounded.

The fortyish shop assistant had considerable experience of exploiting the unease of males who entered her domain to purchase an intimate garment for a wife or lady friend. This entrant seemed even more unnerved than was usual and she obviously felt there were good pickings to be had. Before the Guv'nor really had time to gather his wits he was talked into buying a pair of scarlet, frilly French knickers for an astronomical sum. 'Straight from one of the best fashion houses in Paris. Your wife will simply adore them, sir.'

No one could have been more surprised than the recipient of the gift at Christmas. I don't think she ever accepted his explanation of the circumstances leading up to this rash purchase, and in consequence was probably always suspicious of it being a sop to conscience.

While his friends thought the incident hilarious, the Guv'nor was not so happy. Comprehending the Major's tactics that had led to this unexpected and expensive purchase, he went round making threatening noises about solicitors' letters if a cheque were not soon forthcoming for the hay. Nothing ever was done about it as, on sober reflection, it must have been appreciated that the cost of solicitors' action would probably be far more than the £5 value of the load of hay.

On the Thursday afternoon before Easter I was cycling down the road when I saw Sodding Sykes come out of a field gateway ahead. He waited for me to reach him and called out, 'Hey lad, seen my horse? Slipped the rein at the Old Rectory. Can't find it anywhere.'

Well, that is the gist of what he said, with all the profanities removed. His language was so laced on this occasion that I had difficulty in understanding what he was saying. To say the least, he was a trifle agitated, and his nose and cheeks were a deeper shade of puce. From the further verbal outflow I deduced that he had tied his chestnut's reins to the gate of the Old Rectory, and when he came out after visiting, an hour and a half later, the horse was gone. He obviously had not tied it securely. Yes, I would phone his home if I saw the horse, and having made my promise I cycled on.

That night the Bobby phoned the Guv'nor. 'Major Sykes has lost his horse, couldn't find it anywhere, thinks someone has stolen it. Would we keep an eye out.' By chance, overhearing the Guv'nor's response, I thought he was being just a little too matter-of-fact. And when he suggested to the Bobby that it might be one of Sodding Sykes' friends having a little joke my suspicions were aroused. It was well known in the village that the Major regularly visited the Old Rectory almost every Thursday afternoon. The lawyer who lived there was always in London on Thursdays, and his wife was one of the ladies who favoured Sodding Sykes, 'A real card and such fun' was her reported opinion. From the road gate the curving drive up to the house was lined with laurels and the building was hidden from the road by trees and shrubbery, predominantly evergreens. Conversely, the road was hidden from the house. Anyone aware of Sodding Sykes' habits would have ample time to lead the horse away. Even so, while the Old Rectory stood in an isolated position, other dwellings were not far away in both directions so a horse thief was unlikely to have gone far without one of our arrow-eyed local housewives seeing. It wasn't at all like the Guv'nor to engage in such activities, but next day I did check out every likely building on the farm that could hide a horse.

I also happened to be around to eavesdrop when the Bobby pedalled into the yard to see the Guv'nor. Sodding Sykes was now firmly convinced the animal had been stolen and wanted the County Constabulary alerted. The Bobby, who never did warm to the Major's patronising attitude towards him, had also suggested that he notify his police colleagues to watch those establishments that specialised in equine steaks. This sounded to me very much like turning the knife in the wound. One almost began to feel sorry for Sodding Sykes.

Easter came and went. On Tuesday morning Wully was pedalling flat-footedly to work when, on rounding the corner near the Old Rectory, he was confronted with the Major's chestnut mare tied up to the drive gate. While he was all for getting the Guv'nor to phone the police with the news, the Guv'nor advised against this, suggesting that if Wully was first with the news the Law might think he or we had something to do with the disappearance. Anyway, Sodding Sykes and his horse were soon reunited.

There were many suspects for this assumed practical joke, and the great mystery was where the horse had been hidden over the weekend. Knowing the Guv'nor's moods and his rather smug, nonchalant air whenever the subject was raised, I knew that if he were not actually the instigator he knew more than he was telling. Particularly when, about a week later, Sodding Sykes' cheque came through the post and the Guv'nor was convulsed with laughter.

As can be imagined, Sodding Sykes did not really appreciate the three-day absence of his horse and made some remarkably crude suggestions, which were both physically and biologically impossible, as to what he would do to whoever was responsible if apprehended.

Not much more than 12 months later Sodding Sykes sold his mansion and moved north. One can speculate that the growing reluctance of tradesmen to give him credit or to part with any goods other than for cash made life rather difficult. On top of this, one or two of his middle-aged lady friends had finally realised that the decanter, not themselves, was the object of his visits. The bungalow with smallholding which he purchased in Norfolk was better suited to the health of his bank balance while still allowing him to ride to hounds and swear his way comfortably through life.

In fact, he has recently sworn his last on this earth. He wasn't really a bad soul, so I shouldn't think he's stoking the fires. But if he is, I bet he can outswear Old Nick.

***

The cattle haulier was in the yard the other day to collect some bullocks for market. 'Did you hear old Sodding Sykes is dead?' he asked. I nodded. 'That was a rum trick your old man and mine played on him, wasn't it?' he continued with a laugh. 'Don't tell me you didn't know about it?' My look of incredulous amazement prompted this last remark.

From what was then related I can now piece together the answers to the mystery of 40 years past. My informant's father, the previous haulier, could not get paid for taking Sodding Sykes' horse to the Waveney Hunt and back. This had been mentioned to the Guv'nor, and between the two of them they hatched a plan.

The cattle haulier knew a riding stable at Newmarket which at holiday times had more custom than it had horses available. The owner of the establishment would be happy to pay for the loan of an extra horse over the Easter holiday. The haulier was sure he could find just the right docile beast needed.

As expected, Sodding Sykes made his usual Thursday visit to the Old Rectory, and as soon as he was in the house and the coast was clear the Guv'nor, lurking nearby, took the horse into one of his fields, where the haulier's lorry was waiting behind a couple of wheat ricks. The lorry was off and probably nearly to Newmarket by the time the Major, thirst quenched, doodled down the Old Rectory drive.

On Easter Monday evening the horse was collected by the haulier from Newmarket, and very early the next morning unloaded and tied up from whence it had been snatched. From the riding stable owner's payment the Guv'nor was able to take £5 for his hay and the haulier enough to cover for the outstanding trip to the hunt, as well as the cost of going to Newmarket a couple of times. No wonder the Guv'nor had looked so smug when the Major eventually paid up for the hay.

I suggested to the present haulier that as payment had already been made perhaps the cheque should have been returned. 'Good Heavens, no' he retorted, climbing back into the cab of his lorry. 'They needed that for the sodding interest, didn't they!'

Bloody Hay!

'I HAVE something in my eye. Can you see it?' Mrs Probert put a delicately manicured index finger to her right eyelid and gently pushed it up. Feeling somewhat responsible as it was my hay bales we were moving, the invitation was accepted.

'There is a hay fragment in the corner. Must be a piece of leaf. If you can make the eye water it will probably float out,' I observed, soothingly.

'My hankie is in the left pocket. You could use the corner to dab the thing out.' It was more an order than a request, so I did as instructed.

'I'm not very good at this sort of thing. My hand isn't very steady.' Frankly, one feels a bit awkward in such circumstances.

'Think you've got it. Yes, that feels better. The eye is really watering now.' Indeed, big tears were rolling down her right cheek. It was just then that my wife appeared to tell me I was wanted on the telephone. No wonder she looked a bit surprised. A woman in tears and me standing there with a handkerchief.

Mrs Probert was collecting ten bales of hay in her Range Rover for her horse. If she had just let me load it instead of trying to help, this sort of incident would have been avoided. Bloody hay!

There is this myth about hay that the uninitiated nourish, that it is soft and wholesome stuff in which one can have a lot of fun – "making hay" means having a good time. In reality it is loathsome, itchy, dusty material. It sticks to your clothes and gets into your boots, and it is distributed all over the house when you take them off. Good hay is supposed to be sweet smelling, but it can block your nose, make you wheeze and cough, get into your eyes, and have you scratching all over your anatomy. As for "making hay" in the fun sense, the only time I embarked on an amorous adventure with a girl in a haystack she started to sneeze and couldn't stop. That episode was short-lived.

Having a lifetime's experience of haymaking, there is no doubt in my mind that it is the most tortuous task in agriculture to get it safely gathered in without spoiling. Hay has this remarkable affinity with rain; there can be prolonged summer drought, but cut grass for hay and the heavens will open. No wonder all the cattle keepers have turned to ensiling grass, and we would too if horses could be fed on the stuff. Horses eat hay and this is the market we supply, the riding fraternity who are predominantly female.

The affinity between horses and the fair sex is difficult to understand, if not past understanding. However, hay they want for their steeds, so hay they shall have. The trade is not so bad when a lady wants a cartload of bales at a time. Unfortunately, many of the horsy ladies don't have the storage to take more than a few bales at once, which means extra work for us. Most have car trailers and take 20 or more at a time, but Mrs Probert can only manage what she can squeeze into the back of her Range Rover.

Mrs Probert lives at Bergholt and is married to a bit of a "stuffed shirt" who works in the City. He does, however, provide handsomely for his wife, who is exceedingly County Sloan with obligatory Barbour jacket, Burberry skirt and Hunter green wellies for country tasks such as handling a few bales of hay. She arrives in the farmyard looking as if she has just been removed from one of those glossy adverts for rural attire that are found in *The Field* and *Country Life*, with beautifully styled hair and blemishless make-up. One would not call her pretty; striking, yes. She reminds me of her grandmother, Mrs Ludington-Witt, who resided in this parish for most of her life.

The next occasion Mrs Probert arrived in the yard for hay, it again fell to me to struggle to get the bales out of the dutch barn and into the back of her vehicle. As usual she insisted on helping.

'Ouch! There are some thistles in this bale.' She was examining the palm of her left hand. 'I think the prickles are still there. Can you have a look? I've left my spectacles at home. Have a job seeing small things.'

The hand was presented, so I held it and quickly saw a couple of small thistle spines. During the process of retrieving them Tim drove by in his tractor. Happening to glance up at him there was no mistaking a smirk on that ruddy face of his. The sort of comment that would be passed on as soon as he saw one of the other men came to mind, 'Just seen the boss hand in hand with that smart bit of goods who comes for hay.' Perhaps I was being unnecessarily sensitive but I there and then decided that next time Mrs Probert appeared in the yard someone else could attend to her needs.

It so happened that when the Range Rover next purred into the farm her husband was at the wheel. 'Felicity's seeing our youngster off on a skiing holiday in Austria. Got the chore of collecting the hay for her nag. Nearly out of the stuff.'

Had his wife come for the hay bales I would have kept to my decision to have one of our men do the work. I did not want another of those little intimate incidents which made me ripe for leg pulling. Silly, I know, because Mrs Probert was unlikely to keep getting dust in her eyes or prickles in her fingers. Still, with a hardy male, no problem.

Mr Probert was telling me about his skiing progress and pulling bales in a heap for me to convey when he somehow stumbled. 'Ouch, God I've ricked my ankle.' He sat down on a bale and started to examine his left ankle.

I nearly exclaimed, 'I don't believe this!' We never had any such problems with other hay customers. The Proberts must be accident prone. After feeling his ankle and flexing it around, Mr Probert concluded that there was no more damage than a sprain. I completed loading the Range Rover and he hobbled back to the driver's seat, insisting he would have no problem getting home and declining my offer to drive him there.

Out of courtesy, and concern for my Public Liability insurance policy, I phoned the Proberts the following evening to ask about Mr

Probert's ankle. Mrs Probert answered; 'Just a little swollen and sore; nothing to worry about. You naughty man, fancy pushing the poor fellow over just because you were so upset that I didn't come for the hay.' There were gales of laughter. She was only "taking the mickey", true. Even so, I didn't laugh with enthusiasm.

***

'Well, what sort of fun are we going to have today?' A beaming Mrs Probert skipping gaily down from her Range Rover. There had been a storm during the night and Tim and Toby were across the field sawing up a fallen willow that had blocked the brook, causing floodwater to run into an adjoining meadow. With no one else in the farmyard the hay bale handling task again fell to me.

'With all due respect, you and your husband are accident prone on this place. I'm not going to let you touch a bale today.' The message was conveyed in jocular fashion, even if I really meant it. At least Mrs Probert had a sense of humour, even if she did overdo the laughter. As I hauled the bales out of the barn and loaded them, there was the usual chit-chat. Her husband's ankle was fine now. Carrying out the fifth bale my feet suddenly went from under me and down I went onto my rear end. The slush on the concrete after the heavy rain obviously contained something extra slippery.

Mrs Probert was convulsed with laughter. I wasn't. The slush was sloppy enough for the water to soak immediately through my trousers. Pushing the hay bale away I attempted to get up. Mrs Probert extended a helping hand. At the moment I took it that stupid thought of 'If anyone sees this I'll never live it down' struck and spurred me to get back on my feet even faster than I was endeavouring to do. Regrettably, the extra spurt of effort overcame caution and the next thing one of my feet had slipped away again and I was down on my back. Only this time Mrs Probert came with me as I still had hold of her hand. The heady fragrance of Chanel No 5 simply induced near panic to my efforts to get back on my feet. Fortunately Mrs Probert had landed on top of me and did not appear to have come into contact with any of the slush. She was near hysterical with laughter.

I could feel water trickling down the back of my legs as the remaining bales were loaded.

'I'm having a dinner party tonight. It will make a lovely tale to tell my guests how Mr Freeman fell for me!' More laughter, 'and I will be able to say it is the first time I've ever made a man wet himself.' She laughed so much her tears spoiled that immaculate make-up.

I tried to laugh too. Not very convincingly. Bloody hay!

The County Show

AS THE countryside has become a pretty place to live rather than a food factory, change has affected cherished institutions like county shows. Once purely the domain of the agricultural fraternity and its hangers-on, the event now caters for the whole county community and entices the town dweller as well.

To the traditional main ring events have been added turns that once were confined to circuses, while every commercial enterprise in the area appears to have a corner to tout its wares; one is just as likely to find a stand selling girlie videos as one selling gumboots. Currently there are more cars sold than tractors, and certainly more on display. Perhaps, nowadays, there is so much entertainment of one kind or another that the County Show does not hold the same expectancy or provide the same degree of enjoyment for me that it did when agriculture ruled supreme. Or is it just another case of nostalgia? Great times were had...and surely there can never be a show to compare with the one when the Guv'nor' took Billy Hastings.

Billy Hastings was a neighbouring farmer and pretty much the Guv'nor's henchman. Whenever the Guv'nor made his annual trip to vote against whatever the Milk Marketing Board proposed at its annual meeting, Billy went too. On other sallies forth against bureaucracy, be it the Tithe Commissioners or the War Ag, Billy was in the supporting role. Likewise if the Guv'nor went on some farmers' outing it was usually as a twosome.

Fundamental in this relationship was Billy's rather restricted upbringing under devout Victorian parents who had little to do with life beyond the farm gate. The worldly Guv'nor was sophisticated by Billy's standards and a willing mentor to his unsure neighbour. Billy would never have had the confidence to undertake these jaunts on his own. This is not to imply he was a shrinking violet, on the contrary, he was a big, amiable man who wouldn't hesitate to call a spade a spade, and a damned good farmer to boot, but on the social scene he was a follower rather than a leader.

Wives usually accompanied husbands to county shows, even though they knew that they would be submerged in agricultural lore, but one year in the mid-fifties the Guv'nor's and Billy Hastings' wives had booked for a coach outing to Kew Gardens on a date that coincided with the first day of the County Show. Thus Billy suggested to the Guv'nor that on this occasion he'd like to come along with him. As I would otherwise have been the Guv'nor's sole companion and given to arguing with him, he was not amiss to Billy accompanying us. Unfortunately from my point of view, we went in Billy's car, a rather grand Morris saloon that had seen better days. The front seats were all right but as the back compartment was regularly used for taking the odd calf to market my perch was not very desirable, despite Billy's gestured, 'I swep all the muck out for you.' Still, I preferred not to take chances and spread several layers of newspaper over the stained back seat before sitting down. Off we went as the half past eight village bus ground up the hill before us.

Perhaps the occupants of the front seat enjoyed the 12-mile journey to the showground; I did not. Two farmers travelling together farm other people's land that they pass. Their talk was largely a series of critical observations, 'Mess old Harold's got in that field, full of poppies ...' 'Why don't Brown get that grass cut. That'll all be run to seed if he leaves it much longer.'...'They're not as good a bunch of heifers as you usually see at Pond Farm. Never been the same since the Scots stockman left.'...And so on.

It was not the comments that were of concern to me but the fact that both men continually directed their gaze to fields beside the road. Every time the Guv'nor made a comment on something we passed, Billy would look too and the car would start to veer across the road. Never have I given such a polished display of back seat driving, for the prospect of drawing my last breath in that machine loomed large on several occasions. At least Billy didn't complain about my cries of 'LOOK OUT!'; his only reaction being to mumble, 'Cor, that was a near one,' and then repeat the performance a few minutes later.

Much to my relief, we did eventually bump into the showground parking field still unharmed. I followed in their wake to the turnstile, the familiar clack, clack of straw pitching machines, the dominant sound at shows in those days, reviving my spirits. Once on the showground I parted from my seniors to wander amongst rows of brightly painted tractors and fantasise about being in the driving seat. Next day our worn, if faithful, tractors at home would be treated with disdain. There was always the hope that the Guv'nor would suddenly be smitten with the desire to buy me a new one, but it never happened.

At noon I made my way to the stand of Rearden and Peeps, corn merchants, with whom the Guv'nor dealt. This was the arranged rendezvous before the three of us moved on to lunch elsewhere. Like other corn merchants at the Show, Rearden and Peeps did little actual business with their clients. To all, this was a public relations exercise, to offer hospitality and have their representatives ingratiate themselves with the callers in the hope of improved business in the future. There were, and still are, those farmers whose only activity at county shows is to pass from one such hospitality tent to the next until the only thing they can then pass is what they have consumed.

The Guv'nor was not one of this ilk and I was therefore surprised, having passed the swarthy rep at the entrance of R & P's (set there by the management to entice the likely and discourage the unlikely) to find the Guv'nor cheerful and Billy Hastings decidedly so, both with a pink gin in hand. It became clear from the chatter that both men must have visited other centres of hospitality before this one. The Guv'nor was talking a lot in a loud voice, a sure sign of alcohol titillation, while Billy laughed at the most inane jokes in an uncontrolled manner, not true to his usual form. It was not like the Guv'nor to go "tent crawling"; I could only conclude that the display of social acceptance was to impress Billy.

At least I wouldn't be getting merry on the fruit cup that filled my glass; the penny-pinching management of R & P knew who gave the orders and wrote the cheques and where the more potent hospitality should be lavished. The Guv'nor had been in the process of entertaining with observations on a London nightclub but quickly changed the subject when I arrived for fear that the tale might be repeated to his wife no doubt. So that was what he got up to when he went to vote against the Milk Marketing Board.

'Well, drink up Billy, we must be off – thank you Mr Rearden, so nice to see you again;' the Guv'nor shook his host's hand during the exchange farewells. As the flap of the tent was lifted for us to depart it was noticeable that Billy's gait was much more rolling that usual. Pondering the thought that Billy wasn't much of a drinking man, I followed behind.

Yes, I'd never seen him do more than sip a single sherry at the Guv'nor's social functions, and I had never seen a bottle of any kind on the Hastings' sideboard.

I thought we were bound for the Country Landowners' Association tent for lunch, but we were obviously in for a detour. The two seniors sidled through a row of shiny blue Fordsons into Ipswich Tractors' caravan. 'We were here earlier,' beamed the Guv'nor for my information. 'Billy's ordered a new Super Major. He just wants to check on something.'

'My God! He must be stoned' was my mental reaction. Billy Hastings always bought secondhand machinery; he was even tighter than the Guv'nor. This just wasn't right. But the whisky bottle was out; no, they didn't want another tipple, but in the end they both did. There was no offer to me, not that I wanted one. Eventually we moved on.

'Think I've had enough; shouldn't have had that last one,' Billy confided ruefully to the Guv'nor.

'Nonsense, enjoy yourself, it's all free; get some of the money back they take off us,' cheered the Guv'nor as at last we headed for the CLA lunch tent. The Guv'nor was a CLA member solely because they had the only really good lunches on the showground. The other diners in the tent were not really of his class, the majority appearing to be very county, or very horsy, or both. Far too many extreme Oxford accents chuntered on about the smoked salmon and the bouquet of the Beaujolais; to be honest, I never felt comfortable in such company, but the fare was very good.

No doubt the Guv'nor was out to further impress Billy, who had never ventured into the CLA domain before and was far too happy to feel the pangs of unease that I did among the predominant local upper crust. I cannot now recall what was ordered from the waitress or eaten that day because of my preoccupation with Billy's antics. To begin with he had asparagus soup and, ignoring the correct utensil, proceeded to slop it into his mouth with his dessert spoon, accompanied by the most extraordinary sucking noises. This performance even sobered the Guv'nor up a little – who enquired, 'Having trouble Billy?'

'Tha's my top plate. I have a job with soup, but tha's lovely stuff this.'

I think there was more soup on his chin than in his mouth. The noise drew looks of unease from neighbouring tables. It was a relief when the last slurp came, but worse was to follow. He seemed to be having trouble in cutting up his main course. I guessed what was going to happen to the pile of peas on his plate, and I was right. The knife slipped and the peas were scattered, but I had not anticipated that they would travel so far. A cascade fell across the neighbouring table, most garnishing a plate of sherry trifle. A rather elegant lady was poised with spoon at that moment: the expression on her face was unmistakably one of mild shock.

'Your peas have just landed on my wife's dessert' scolded her husband. 'Sorry about that – but I won't charge yer for them!' Billy responded and laughed at his own wit. The gentleman at the next table was obviously taken aback by this brazen response and sat speechless until asking the waitress to get his wife an unsullied plate of trifle.

I noticed the Guv'nor was displaying pronounced unease at his friend's conduct, not least by being over-generous by his pouring of the wine into my glass and not topping up Billy's. Billy had strawberries and ice cream for dessert, and while he did not distribute this on others he did manage to knock most of the ice cream into his own lap with his elbow when reaching across the table for the sugar. More hearty laughter as the ice cream was scooped out of the lap by hand and put back on the plate, 'Can't afford to waste this beauty.'

Then he spilt his wine; by the time the meal was finished the mess on the table looked as if a one-year-old had been let loose. The Guv'nor was obviously embarrassed, for he soon hustled us out after completing our meal. Billy seemed blissfully happy, though not at all steady on his pins. When we passed through the portal it was necessary to squeeze by a party of latecomers waiting outside the tent for a table. Billy went too far wide; I saw him trip over a guy rope and topple on to the side of the tent. There was an almighty sound of rending canvas and Billy disappeared from sight; well, except for one foot held at the bottom of the tear. We were left looking at the sole of Billy's boot. The hubbub of conversation inside the tent came to an abrupt halt, silence reigned. No doubt most were, to say the least, surprised at this dramatic re-entry of the tipsy diner. The silence was broken by a roar from Billy of 'What silly bugger put that rope there. I might have broken my f...... neck!'

Now I am sure that in the privacy of his own farmyard Billy Hastings might have been given to expressing a few obscenities, but I had never heard him do so there or anywhere; not even the odd swear word. This was quite out of character, albeit that the circumstances were unusual. The Guv'nor and I stood in amazement with the rest of those outside, probably trying to pretend that Billy had nothing to do with us. After a few seconds the foot was withdrawn into the tent and shortly thereafter Billy's ruddy countenance was thrust through the tear in the tent's side; he was departing the way he had come.

Unfortunately he could muster no more grace in his exit, for having got one foot out, he tripped again, landing flat on his face before us. At least we were spared another flow of invective and both the Guv'nor and I would willingly have slunk further into the little crowd that had by then gathered if Billy had not commanded, 'Well, come on then, give me a bloody hand up.' We did and hustled him away as quickly as we could.

'Are you feeling all right, Billy?' the Guv'nor asked as we progressed along an avenue.

'I'm feelin' a little queasy,' Billy responded. Indeed, he was now looking decidedly pale and drawn, his normal puce complexion having faded. The Guv'nor decided that we had better forego a further look round the Show and make tracks for the car park. Billy was looking decidedly ill. Regrettably we should have sat him down somewhere and not tried to reach the car park right then. Regrettably because when we reached the narrow exit passage beside the pay booth Billy became very ill indeed. It required an attendant to bring two fire buckets full of sand before the route was again passable.

Billy felt a little better after that. I pointed out to the Guv'nor that Billy was in no fit state to drive home and, for that matter, perhaps he had imbibed a little too much as well. At first indignant at my suggestion, the Guv'nor finally agreed to let me drive.

Having retrieved the car keys, we bundled Billy into the back of the Morris – he certainly wouldn't notice the stink of the calves. The Guv'nor hardly said a word on the way home, no doubt feeling a tinge guilty at having not discouraged his friend's appreciation of pink gins and whisky. I rather enjoyed the drive, for once being in a commanding position, so to speak.

I heard that when Billy had recovered he cancelled the new tractor he had ordered at the Show. I don't think he ever did buy a new one before he retired. He continued to go on jaunts with the Guv'nor for many years, but the Guv'nor never took him to the County Show again.

Bettering the Gentry

'I SEE Great Longham Hall is up for sale again. Them people what had it as a hotel has gone broke, so they say. Great owd place like that ain't no good to nobody nowadays.'

Old Newson lowered his rear end slowly on to the straw bale beside me as he spoke. A strong easterly wind had driven us both into the barn on a wild November day, and even there there were sufficient draughts to chill. A pile of bales in one corner, which were awaiting collection by a horsy lady, afforded a cosy relief and for once I had no pressing desire to escape from whatever subject was Harry Newson's "flavour of the day".

'The taxes and upkeep on a mansion like that would be a drain on a millionaire's pocket,' I suggested.

'Expect the owd council will snap it up for offices or an owd folks home; then you and me will be meetin' the bill. I never did go a mucher on the gentry, but they was the right sorts for them grut big places. When I was at Great Longham Hall there were fourteen of us at work there for Sir Hubert Prigmore. Let me see, there were the butler, housekeeper, cook, head gardener and two under-gardeners, a chauffeur, a groom, a handyman, a backhouse boy and four maids.' There was a suggestion of nostalgia in the sage's words; I had not previously heard him mention this employment in his colourful life.

'I didn't know you worked for the Prigmores. That must have been some years ago.'

'Right, that was a few years ago. First job I ever had. I was the backhouse boy – did all the odd jobs – got the sticks for the fires, filled the coal scuttles, polished the shoes, carried for the cook and the butler. I were there about three year. Right good times they were too.'

'Good? I thought being in service in those days was really hard.'

''Course, you got ordered around, but if you played your cards right that weren't that hard work. You could near get away with murder and the gentry wouldn't know nothin' about it. Blast man, the butler and the cook had got all that place sewn up. That were the same in most of them big houses. The gentry didn't know what was going on and so long as you "yes sirred" and "yes ma'amed" them they was happy. You'd never believe what went on behind their backs, but you has to as I'm now goin' to tell you as soon as I got me coat collar turned up to keep me owd neck from chillin'. You won't want me to go all husky so you couldn't hear what I'm saying?' There were many occasions I would have been quite happy not to be able to hear what he was rambling on about. However, for once I was quite intrigued to hear about his service at Great Longham Hall.

'Let me see, that must have been 1918 when I went there. I was 14 or 15 and just out of school. Old Sir Hubert were still alive then and the young one had just come back from the war. The old feller was beginning to flag. Like most of them gentry, he'd spent the best part of his life huntin', drinkin' and womanizing and that were catching up on him. Got so he couldn't get a leg over a horse or lift a glass of wine to his mouth, so stands to reason he were gettin' past gettin' his owd hormones excited enough to do a woman a good turn. About six months after I started at the Hall the owd man popped off. Had a stroke while he was out in the garden one morning, only her ladyship were away and they didn't notice Sir Hubert was missing until evening. Found him face down in a bed of catmint with his little owd legs tucked forward under him and his right thumb stuck halfway up his nose, like as how he'd been pickin' it when he collapsed. O' course, that rigor mortis had set in and they couldn't straighten him out proper; no one could when he were alive, so they weren't a'goin' to now, were they?'

There followed a brief interlude for mirth and, sure enough, out came a spotted handkerchief which was dabbed at his mouth before old Newson continued.

'Now that weren't much of a thing for her ladyship to come home and find the owd feller on the bed with his head between his legs and his thumb stuck up his nose like he was cockin' a snook, was it? Well, the head gardener, he were a heady fellow, had the idea of gettin' a bunch of carnations and puttin' in the owd boy's hand that was half up his snout so as it would look as if he were takin' a snifty when his lights went out. Then the butler and the housekeeper slipped a bolster cover over each leg and pulled the old bedspread up high and you wouldn't have known the old feller weren't lying in state. The young one became the next Sir Hubert but he were a bit namby pamby, like a lot of them gentry are. Too soft a livin' so after a while they breed soft. They say that when he was in the army they made him into an officer because he was a Sir, but then reckoned he was more of a problem than the enemy so they gave him the job of defending Loch Lomond. Anyways, some actress got her hands on him and they was goin' to be wed. She were a good looker, but she properly threw her weight about. None of us liked her. The cook particularly. On the wedding day the cook laced Sir Hubert's porridge with Epsom Salts. During the service, when they got to the part where the owd vicar say "for better or worse", Sir Hubert says, "Excuse me" and without another word ran from the church. Tha's the gentry for you again. A workin' feller would just have come right out with it, "Hold you hard Vicar, I've been taken short". Most gals would have been thinkin' he didn't want to go through with it and would have left the church too. Not her, she wasn't going to lose being Her Ladyship, and there she stands 'til Sir Hubert comes back, him all sheepish like. Same thing happened again 'fore they signed the register. When they come back from their honeymoon the new ladyship proper put her foot down, but she didn't get the better of us. Her maid was always getting an earful. One day she heard her ladyship telling a friend she didn't want any nippers. So when the Prigmores is away visitin' this maid goes to Sir Hubert's dressing table drawer where he keep his rubber johnies – they call 'em condemns now – and she takes out a couple of dozen packets, steamed them open and puts a pinhole you know where, sticks the flap down again and puts them back with the other packets. She said there were several gross. Expect Sir Hubert had bought a job lot; he always got an eye cocked for a good bargain. Anyways, afore the year was out the maid was a'grinnin' 'cause she'd found out her ladyship was puddin'd. I don't know much about these things but they tell me them little owd sperms is like a bunch of hungry steers lookin' for a weak place in the fence. Well, the nipper is born but her ladyship weren't a'goin' to feed it, not her, she want to keep her figure. Tha's all right for us men to laugh about it but it ain't no laughin' matter to have a nipper a pullin' and a chompin' away at yer lallies. Just you look at Bramble Blake's missus, time she'd had her thirteenth hers was near stretched to her knees. People think she's a flat-chested hunchback but they're wrong. What she do is push her lallies back over her shoulder under her jumper so they ain't no trouble when she's a bendin' for housework or spud pickin'. Clever woman her. Anyhows, as I was sayin', her ladyship weren't goin' to feed the nipper so she have a nursemaid. She was goin' around telling all her snooty friends what a good little feller the nipper is. O' course she don't know the nursemaid is putting a swig of gin in its feedin' bottle to keep it quiet.

'Her ladyship was always complaining about the food. One time she sent the soup back sayin' it needed more spice. The cook soon spiced that up and sent it back. Still weren't up to her ladyship's liking, so when it came back again the cook got all of us to have a go. It didn't come back again!'

I resisted the temptation to elicit an explanation of spicing; and in any case there was no stopping old Newson now.

'Her Ladyship had one of those simonize cats.'

'Don't you mean Siamese?' I interjected, knowing full well he would say: 'Tha's what I said. Anyways, that were always bein' a nuisance to the cook and the scullery maid. One day the butler found it dead in the game pantry. The cat had tried to jump up and get one of the hares or pheasants that were hangin' from the top shelf, only that didn't quite make it and got its head through the trussing twine that was looped on a hook and hung itself. Well, they knew there

would be a row about lettin' the cat get in the pantry when Her Ladyship heard about it, so it was decided to say nothing. The cook saw her chance. "We ain't got enough hares to go round at the dinner party tonight and they'll be so sozzled with wine they won't know the difference". The rest of 'em didn't need more tellin'. The handyman soon had that cat skinned and that evening that were in the pot with the hares. Of course, you can be sure that the butler saw to it that Her Ladyship got the portion what was the cat. She sent word down after the meal that she thought the hare should have hung a bit longer! We all laughed. That cook was always feedin' Her Ladyship stuff you wouldn't give a cat but that never seemed to do her no harm. Sometimes she went a little too far. I remember Her Ladyship sending back some curried prawns with a note saying that they tasted like something that had been got from the stable. All the cook did was grin and say, "She ain't far wrong". She were a rare tartar were that cook.'

'You don't expect me to believe all that,' I said, and then recalling how this challenge was usually met, as again on this occasion, with a hurt: 'Now would I tell you a lie? Anyways, most of us at the hall had a racket. The head gardener kept lots of folk supplied with fruit and vegetables on the quiet; when flowers were cut for the hall the gardeners would snip extra ones and they'd find their way to a flower stall in Ipswich. Sir Hubert and his mates got through a fair few bottles of wine when there was a dinner. When the guests started to get a bit merry the owd butler would start watering down the refill bottles. He, the cook and the housekeeper had their own booze-up later with what had been put on the side. The wages may not have been much in those days but there were plenty of perks for the takin' at the Hall. Didn't do no harm to the Prigmores; they got all they needed.'

'Maybe,' I scolded, 'but it was still dishonest. No wonder they eventually couldn't afford to keep the place going.'

'The dodges didn't do 'em no harm. It were her.'

'Her?'

'Her Ladyship. Sir Hubert were always trying his luck with the maids, just like most of the gentry did. Course, most of them girls had their heads screwed on the right way, they knew what he was after. Anyways, one of 'em gets herself in the family way elsewhere, so she thinks that if she encourages Sir Hubert she can say he's the father and get a bit of money out of him for the nipper when it arrives. Only she tells one of the other maids what she's up to; daft ha'peth. This other maid is a God-fearin' girl and thinks it's a wicked scheme. She tells Her Ladyship and, as you might be guessin', Her Ladyship catches Sir Hubert and the puddin'd maid at it. Now in the old days the ladyships didn't worry about their old boys playin' around on the side, kept 'em happy. So they'd turn a blind eye. But not this one, she weren't from gentry stock, her father had been a tax inspector, and it must have rubbed off on her for she were after all she could get. Straight away she's in for a divorce. Took Sir Hubert for thousands, so they say. Anyways, he couldn't afford to keep the Hall goin' after that, so he sold up and moved away. Old place were empty for several years.'

'What about the pregnant maid. Did she get any money out of him?'

'No, Sir Hubert weren't that soft. He'd got his condemns, hadn't he?'

'What happened to the maid then?' I persisted.

'She married the fellow responsible. Well, I must be gettin' home, my old dog will be waitin' for his tea.'

I thought old Newson's response decidedly sheepish. Particularly when he ignored my further question whether he knew who the fellow was. I suppose it could have been that he did not hear due to the noise of the gale as he slid open the barn door.

The Confession

IT IS a common misapprehension among urban dwellers that the countryside offers anonymity. Seclusion, yes; but anonymity rarely. In a small village the major preoccupation and pleasure in life is knowing who everyone is and what they are about. With some folk this is a practised art, and their intelligence gathering reaches a standard of which any nation's secret service would be proud.

It has always been very difficult to conceal anything from eyes and ears in one's own village; thus he or she who contemplates any action which they desire to keep hidden had best go far afield; logic which probably led to the well-known saying about fouling one's own doorstep.

This must have been the considered practice of a well-to-do farmer in the neighbouring parish, a man wealthy enough not to soil his hands in manual work and having a foreman to perform the day-to-day administration of the large farm. The farmer's energies were directed elsewhere. He was a pillar of the local chapel and a parish and rural district councillor, as well as being prominent in several of the county's charitable organisations. However, most of his energy appears to have been directed at the fair sex. His womanising activities were extraordinarily discreet, for he was intent on maintaining a reputation of unblemished respectability.

At times it must have caused him some mental anguish to reconcile his extra-marital activities with his otherwise pious outlook and behaviour. One can but suppose he was a victim of over-active hormones. Apparently his exploits remained unknown to the village gossips of the time, the earlier part of this century, chiefly because he did not dilly or dally in the immediate neighbourhood.

The farmer's appetite, to say nothing of his stamina, was prodigious in that for the better part of 30 years he regularly called on three ladies. This was achieved under the cover of attending market in three different towns, although little time was actually spent at the market place. In this way his home-loving wife was oblivious of the goings-on.

In addition, there were more casual liaisons at distant venues, particularly with two "professional" ladies in London, the city which he often had to visit in the course of pursuing one of his charitable interests or in connection with his investments. He certainly invested heavily with the "professional" ladies.

The wife was a large, heavy-featured woman, and somewhat plain. One might suppose that because she was wealthy in her own right the union had come about through the farmer's avarice. However, the marriage had all the signs of being happy, and she eventually bore him two sons. Meanwhile the farmer's activities elsewhere produced a girl in Ipswich and another in Bury St Edmunds. The third mistress was a married woman and decidedly more careful.

He provided for his illegitimate progeny and was generous to their mothers; cash for cows being transferred to jewellery, presumably without ever appearing on the books. All of which must have eventually put considerable strain on the purse strings in a period when even wealthy farmers had meagre income from their land. However, by dint of much scheming and no doubt prayer, the farmer still managed to maintain his lifestyle.

A major difficulty arose when one of his sons left school and was intent on taking up a farming career. It would not have been a problem but for the young man's insistence that he should accompany his father to market to gain experience – in marketing practice of course. Not much good can be said of Hitler, but he did resolve the farmer's predicament. Both boys volunteered for military service and the conditioning of the officers' mess saw to it that they took up more gentlemanly pursuits in the City on their return to civilian life.

Eventually the strain began to tell, and in the early 'fifties the farmer, then of similar age, suffered a severe stroke. Although he made a recovery this warning of his own mortality brought a desire to purge his sins, to put him in better stead with his Maker. Thus, rashly, the wife was called to the bedside and asked forgiveness for thirty years of his "carrying on" with other women, and for the fact that this had resulted in a girl in Ipswich and another born in Bury St Edmunds. 'All those surplus women after the slaughter of the Great War. I was simply doing them a favour,' was his audacious excuse.

We do not know if he were surprised by his wife's remarkable composure as she listened to the detailed confession, but he was more than surprised when she soothingly informed him that she was very relieved to hear these revelations. On those days when he had been away at market or in the big city, life had been so boring she had found excitement with certain gentlemen of the neighbourhood. The result of her own adulterous behaviour, she said, was the two sons, each having a different father. The shock to the ailing farmer on hearing this was too much. He there and then had a relapse and expired.

The wife's composure was due to her having previously learned something of her husband's infidelities. This resulted from a visit to the doctor, who informed the understandably stunned woman that she had a non-serious affliction that was only transmitted by certain naughty activity. Nothing was said to the farmer; instead a private investigator was engaged to follow his movements when away from home. Thus the wife learned about the visits to ladies in various places. The investigator was good at his job and also provided the low-down on the children in Ipswich and Bury St Edmunds.

Hell hath no fury .... but the wife's machinations had yet to be finalised before the farmer had his stroke. Of course, the wife had not engaged in promiscuous activities, and there was no truth in her statement that the sons were not her husband's.

Now you, the reader, will be asking yourself how all this is known to the writer, in view of the farmer's successful evasion of the gossips. It seems vengeance was sweet to the wife and she could not refrain from telling her *very* best woman friend in the ±strictest± of confidence, of course, the whole saga. The friend confided in another friend on the understanding that the tale would go no further, and the friend told another friend in great secrecy. And that lady could no more keep it to herself than the others. The story spread and spread until inevitably it became almost common knowledge in the district. I guess there is a moral here somewhere, but I wouldn't dare to retrieve it.

A Little Problem with Cattle

IT MUST have been a year or two after the end of the trouble with old Hitler. One late summer morning Wully cycled into the farmyard and announced, 'The heifers on the Low Meadow have gone. Not one to be seen. I knew they'd get out – you kept them on there too long Guv'nor.'

It was almost an annual event. One could be sure that as the meadows were eaten down, summer drought gradually turning the turf sepia and the flies beginning to worry, some cattle would escape in a quest for peace and lusher pastures. If there were a weak spot in a hedge or fence they would find it and be gone. Invariably this would be at weekends or in the evenings or early mornings, as if the animals knew then there would be few people around the farm to halt their escape. The annual checking of field boundaries for weaknesses appeared to have no effect on preventing these getaways. I do not believe a single year went by without such an event. Returning the cattle from whence they had come was never an easy matter, inevitably requiring much chasing about which produced puffed and panting pursuers, not to mention some very fruity language.

On this particular occasion the Guv'nor despatched all the farm labour, other than Clive the cowman, to locate the beasts. A rotted post and trampled barbed wire indicated the breakout point, but the drought-hard surface of the field beyond provided no clues as to the path the seven young heifers had taken. We were posted in different directions, Rue and Archie towards high-hedged Friars Lane, which wound up the hill on the far side of the field, the Guv'nor and Wernie, the former German prisoner of war, to the wood in the opposite direction, and Wully and myself straight ahead up the valley. As expected, we had hardly crossed the field before Wully was moaning on about people who did not check fences properly and giving his opinion that the heifers should have been put on another pasture weeks ago. Wully's flat-footed gait was the explanation for this tetchiness; walking anywhere was a chore. At the first opportunity I crossed the brook that runs up the valley to the west, giving as my reason that it would be easier to see around to the north as the overgrown hedge and trees that bordered the stream obscured our view from the southern side. In fact, it was more to escape from Wully's grumblings.

The long foliage on the north side was still damp with dew and the bottom of my trousers quickly started to pick up the moisture. To prevent this I moved from the field edge into the crop of near ripe oats, using the headland water furrow in which only the odd oat had taken root so that my progress was not unduly impeded. Wully had slackened his pace on the other side of the brook; at least I could no longer hear him murmuring curses nor see him through the occasional gappy part of the hedge or where it gave way to a flourish of sallows.

The boundary of the oat field was also the farm boundary, and it was necessary to force my way through some straggly hawthorns into the meadow beyond. This was Billy Hastings' property, about five acres of roughish grazing, rectangular in shape, that ran lengthways from the brook up the valley hill to the little road beyond. Two shorthorns stood at the top of the hill watching my progress. In view of my not particularly difficult breaching of the boundary hedge, I intended to advise Billy Hastings that some barbed wire was needed, otherwise his cattle would soon be in our oats. Admittedly the meadow was still quite lush near the brook and there was also ample feed higher up the hill, but digestive fulfilment did not necessarily subdue the bovine desire to travel.

Our own escapees had obviously not come this way, but I was disinclined to clamber through the foliage back across the brook; solitude was preferred to Wully's company. At the far side of

Hastings' meadow a footpath came down the hedge from the road and led across a rather precarious wooden footbridge to our side of the stream. Even though it was not yet 9 am the July sun was beginning to play upon the pool below, from which a faint mist was rising. Wild watercress borders lay between the bank and the main flow of the brook. A mental note was made of its abundance.

My dreamy enjoyment of the stream beneath the footbridge was disturbed by a distant shout. At first I thought it came from the meadow I had just left, but there was no one in sight and the two shorthorns were no longer to be seen, having moved over to the brow of the hill towards the road no doubt. Again the shout, and this time I realised it was Wully, way up on the hill on our side of the brook, waving his arms for me to follow.

By the time I had reached the crest of the hill, which required a detour round the field edge as it was waving ripening barley, Wully had moved on. However, from the field gate into Friars Lane I could see the rest of our stalwarts endeavouring to head off the errant cattle in the clover ley way across the next dip in the landscape. I set off at a trot down Friars Lane, expecting to overtake Wully. As this did not occur I concluded, correctly, that he had chosen a more convoluted route in the hope that by the time he eventually caught up with the rodeo the situation would be under control. It took me a good five minutes to traverse the rutted surface of Friars Lane and, as I had feared, the heifers, having left the clover field, had gone hurtling along the lane towards the road. And as I also feared, heifers being heifers, they decided to enter the open drive gate to the gentleman's residence that stood at the end of the lane.

The gentleman's residence had once been a farmhouse but had been tarted up by someone from London in the 'thirties as an over-large weekend cottage. The present incumbents were a barrister and his wife, the Bigsby-Crapes. It does not need much imagination to guess what was made of this surname by the usual occupants of the taproom at The Wheelwright's Arms!.

The garden was quite extensive, having taken in the old farm orchard and the walled area that now served as a kitchen plot. I arrived just in time to see the thundering herd evade Rue's and

Archie's efforts to divert them and thunder across the immaculate lawn. My mind conjured up a vision of the Guv'nor making abject apology and promising recompense for hoof holes and munched greenery.

This usually involved me having to take a wheelbarrow full of molehill soil and fill each individual indentation while the hurt owner breathed fire down my neck. Being the boy, I always got this unenviable task of weathering the tirade against farmers who couldn't contain their cattle. Additionally, a bountiful basket of eggs, cream and a dressed fowl would follow, but never until the hurt owner had vented his or her spleen on the unfortunate hole filler. The gift never failed to restore sweetness and charm to the scene. It looked as if the gift basket, when it was delivered, would carry a mammoth load for this little lot.

The heifers were hurtling around the garden like a chariot race at the Coliseum. 'Don't chase them. Let them quieten down,' roared the Guv'nor as the beasts plunged through the shrubbery. Rue was just about to say something but only got as far as 'If we .....' I looked to see what had checked him. From the house Mrs Bigsby-Crape had appeared angrily pleading, 'Keep them from my beautiful kitchen garden.'

It was not this plea that had stopped Rue in mid sentence. The lady must still have been enjoying the comfort of her bed when all hell broke loose in the garden below. In her concern she had only thought to don a pair of slippers and had rushed from the house clad only in her nightdress. This certainly covered arms, legs and her almost waistless and bustless torso, but she was either not aware or had forgotten that the white silk material from which it was fashioned was decidedly translucent. It hid all, but nothing.

I have to admit that this lean, fortyish woman in diaphanous trim was my first first-person introduction to female anatomy. Had the woman thought to look at the expressions on five male faces she might have instantly realized something was amiss.

Instead she took off in pursuit of the heifers with a cry of, 'Go away you horrid things,' which was the worst move she could have made, first because the heifers took off again straight through the runner beans and over the kitchen garden; second, because in her anguish she did not see what the animals had just deposited on her lawn. As regards this latter, while we were still present the lady's concern was such she evidently did not notice what was adhering to her slippers.

Fortunately, the animals decided to make exit from the front gate just as quickly as they had entered, and to our mutual amazement and relief turned towards the farm on reaching the road, whereas they could just as easily have gone in the other direction, and heaven knows where to then.

Another piece of luck was Wully's decision, no doubt promoted by his wish to roam no further than absolutely necessary, to cut across to the road from where I had last seen him. Thus he was in position to open a gate into another of our meadows and divert the heifers in as they hustled down towards him. Wully was plainly pleased with his claimed forethought, 'I could see tha's what they were goin' to do. I've bin around cattle long enough to be ahead of 'em.' And for once I think we were all pleased with Wully.

Rue, in his usual crude manner, did not hesitate to inform Wully what he had missed. Of course, the probability that Mrs Bigsby-Crape was so concerned for her garden that she had left her bed without thought of a dressing gown, was not offered. For Rue there could only be a sexual explanation. 'Reckon that husband of hers is past it. So she's lookin' round for another feller to do her some good. Cavorting about in front of us just like an old she cat do when it's trying to entice the toms. Proper upset me I can tell yer.'

And Rue continued to say he was still proper upset for weeks until he had some other stimulating event to pass crude comment about. For all his big talk I noticed he did not volunteer to go and fill in the hoof holes in Mrs Bigsby-Crape's garden that afternoon. Nor did anyone else, despite my protests to the Guv'nor. While I did not entertain Rue's 'She'll have the trousers off you afore you've time to say "Father Christmas",' or any of his other suggestions as to what might be my fate, I was concerned about the earful I would certainly receive concerning damage to the garden.

Luck smiled again, for Mrs Bigsby-Crape's car was not in the garage; she had gone out, probably to the station to meet Mr Bigsby-Crape. The damage was not as bad as I thought it would be, as the only hoof holes were in the kitchen garden, the drought-hard conditions having saved the lawns. After resurrecting the runner beans and scraping the cow pats from a path, I was back out on the road pushing my barrow back to the farm as fast as I could go.

My relief quickly evaporated when a vehicle coming up behind me began to slow to a stop. However, it was not the Bigsby-Crapes about to read the Riot Act but our neighbouring farmer, Billy Hastings.

'What you doing with that barrow up here? Stick it in the van, boy, and I'll give you a lift to the farm.' I accepted; the sooner away from the vicinity of the Bigsby-Crapes' residence the better. Explaining about the heifers breaking out and the rodeo that occurred, I mentioned the two shorthorns in Billy's far field. 'I ain't got no cattle up there boy. I ain't had anything in that field since the spring,' was his response. We concluded that someone else's cattle were wandering and I didn't give it another thought.

However, I did not forget the wild watercress seen that morning. The Guv'nor's wife was particularly partial to watercress, so one evening after work a couple of days later I set off wearing my rubber boots and bearing a small potato sack. In contrast to the fine warm morning when our heifers had broken out, this day had been wet and overcast. It was no longer raining, even if clouds still hung dark and low.

The brook was already slightly swelled by the run-off of the day's rain, and it proved difficult to pluck the watercress without the torrent coming up over the top of my wellingtons. Wading back and forth to place my spoils in the sack which had been left on the wooden footbridge, I chanced to look up the hill in Billy Hasting's meadow, and against a backdrop of inky clouds saw the two shorthorns looking at me. This brought conjecture as to why Billy Hastings had denied having any animals on the field. It was not like him to engage in any illegal activity, but I suspected that these were animals that did not appear on the Ministry returns and were the subject of some deal with a butcher in those days of strict meat rationing. On my next wade back to the sack I was going to look and see if I could tell whether the shorthorns were bullocks or cows, but they had moved away and my curiosity was not up to my walking up the hill to find them.

I knew Archie cycled along the little top road sometimes when he went to see his sister in Longham, so next morning I asked him if he'd seen cattle on Billy Hastings' meadow next to our oat field. His answer was 'not since the spring', and he was fairly sure that there couldn't be anything on that field now as he'd noticed that the gate into the road had been left open. It sounded as if Billy had moved the shorthorns in a hurry. I was even more convinced that there was some sort of illicit goings-on in this connection.

That evening I raised the subject with the Guv'nor. He said that he had seen a couple of shorthorn cows on the field about four weeks ago. He thought it odd as Billy Hastings went in for Ayrshires. The Guv'nor must have mentioned this to Billy at some time during the following weeks and received an assurance that he had no shorthorns nor any cattle on that field since the spring.

The two of them must have speculated that someone in the district was getting a bit of free grazing. If I saw any cattle on there again would I let Billy know immediately. Such clandestine activities were not unknown, particularly when summer droughts set in. Of course, the owner of the cattle always insisted that they had broken out and apologised. In some cases it was a little too pat. The claims that a passer-by must have shut the gate behind the escapees were used a little too frequently not to be suspect. All the same, I still had an uncanny idea that Billy had been up to something. No one reported cattle in the field again during the summer and eventually I assumed the shorthorns had long become roast beef on somebody's plate.

The mystery would probably have been forgotten had there not been another development some six or seven years later. At that time I had a girlfriend from London who was staying at the farm. She was genuinely fascinated by country life, although I am sure the orderly city was more to her liking. Saturday morning was a work period for me and at the Guv'nor's wife's suggestion I planned a footpath route that would give the girl a pleasant walk. When she returned she was quite excited, having seen a green woodpecker for the first time. The location was the trees near the footbridge. She added, 'At first I didn't cross the bridge and follow the path up the field as there were two cows looking at me, but they ran off so I plucked up enough courage to go. I don't know where they went to because when I got to the top of the hill I could not see them anywhere.'

Perhaps it was the inquisition that followed which played a part in the romance cooling. The girl must certainly have wondered if I had some peculiar quirk in requiring so much detail. No, she didn't see which way they ran. Yes, they were sort of brown and white flecked colouring. Yes, they did look like the pictures of shorthorns I showed her. No, she couldn't remember if the gate were open as she used the stile to get into the road. Frankly, I believed the Guv'nor had put her up to this, even though he denied it. And I certainly wasn't going to ask Billy Hastings if he had any brown and white cattle on the meadow.

Once again the mystery was all but forgotten, until the day, years later, when Clive the cowman returned from driving the cows in for milking. 'Blossom made me late. Misses her calf. She'd made a gap in the hedge and was right up the valley blaring away over the far fence. I expect she could see those cattle up on next door's field above the footbridge.' I was thinking about other things and the matter didn't really register until he added, 'Not often you see shorthorns nowadays.'

'How many?' I found myself daring to ask.

'A couple,' and then, seeing the quizzical look on my face, 'Why?'

I ignored his question: 'Were they looking at you. And when you looked again they'd gone?'

'Yes,' he said, puzzled. 'I thought it strange, 'cause since old

Hastings died and Major Whatsit bought that field I've never seen anything grazing there except his horse. Perhaps he's gone in for rare breeds.'

Perhaps I should not have told Clive my experiences, but he was a sensible fellow and I didn't expect him to take the whole thing seriously. Nevertheless, it was not long before the story was making the rounds of the local pubs and not long after that when the first strangers hunting ethereal apparitions arrived. It would all have been very encouraging if it had been a headless horseman or a wayward nun, but ghosts in the form of two shorthorn cows don't have quite the same clout. The footpath through the haunted meadow is now the most trodden in the village, as for every person who is afeared to walk that way because of the mystery, there must be twenty who go hoping to see two bovine ghosts. It would not be so bad if they were red-eyed bulls with foaming nostrils instead of dear old docile doe-eyed shorthorn cows.

Naturally Major Whatsit who owns the field isn't very happy about the traffic and the disturbance to his horse's peace. Personally, believing that the only ghosts are in the mind, I am still convinced there is a rational explanation and that there was some collusion in order to pull my leg. But I'm never going to know now. And as far as I am aware no one has claimed to have seen the bovine spooks since Clive in the mid-seventies.

Only, just when I think the whole thing is in the past something happens. The other night when it was raining the proverbial cats and dogs, I distinctly heard cows mooing. The troubling thing is that we no longer have a dairy herd or any other cattle, nor do any of my neighbours in this valley.

Just A-Measuring the Field

'WOMEN was made to torment men. I don't know what we done wrong that the Good Lord couldn't have made us like worms. Then all we has to do is cut a piece off ourselves and that'd grow into another fellow. Wouldn't be no need for women then.'

One could be sure that sooner or later during the potato picking time Rue would revive this statement as a result of his frustration by the opposite sex. In the days when we grew potatoes they were harvested by gangs of women who went from farm to farm during the season. It was back-aching work, continually stooping to pick up the tubers unearthed by the digging machine, which probably accounts for their moods.

The attraction to casual labour was that earnings were tax-free, payment being in cash, and by moving from farm to farm the Inland Revenue was evaded and avoided. Full names and addresses were rarely given, and any request for same by a farmer was met with the plea from the picker that she was not earning enough to pay any tax, beside which she would not be coming next day so there was no point in giving a name.

None of our farm regulars looked forward to 'tater picking time, and I least of all. It seemed impossible to satisfy the women; there was always something not to their liking. The work was based on so much for a filled sack and, having established and agreed a price, one could be sure that the women would soon be saying it was not enough because the potatoes were too small, or the land too cloddy, or a hundred and one other reasons for complaint.

They preferred to work in defined areas of the field which we stepped out, but you could be sure there would be complaints that the measuring was inaccurate and that somebody had a larger or better patch than the others. They also had a habit of involving members of the farm staff in any disagreement, which could easily have been sorted out among themselves. If one woman had a complaint against another it was rarely aired directly. Instead one of us would be approached to establish whose filled bags were whose, or who had nicked someone's picking pail; the moans seemed endless.

The 'tater pickers never appeared to work with us. One got the impression that the farmer and his men were viewed as if they were an opposing force to be harried and outwitted. It would be unfair to apply dishonest as a generalisation, even if constant vigilance were necessary, but there always seemed to be one picker present who tried a dodge, such as heaping clods and rubbish into the sacks when we were not looking.

Rue, a rural chauvinist, who always fancied himself with the ladies in other circumstances, was given the task of being field master, checking the filled bags and overseeing the loading on to the cart for haulage to the storage barn. Every year he appeared to embrace the task with new fervour. 'I'm going to keep them old gals in order this year. I think I got the master of them now,' was the confident quip, although I knew that by the time the last bag had been carted from the field and the pickers had finally left the scene his deflation would be complete, 'Good riddance. Did ever you see or hear the likes of them? Bloody old women. Hopes we've seen the back of that lot for good.'

Quite probably he had seen the last of most of those who had made up a particular gang, for the composition seemed to change every year and often within a season. I always phoned the same ganger with force requirements, but one never knew how many or who would be in the gang we picked up in a housing estate in the nearby town. Rarely did we have the same ten or a dozen women each day; there always seemed to be a new face and, as sometimes happened, when the gang went elsewhere for a couple of weeks because we did not yet wish to harvest a particular field, when it returned there might be only two or three of the original women left. Usually they were nearly all in the 25-35-year-old age range, urban housewives with children at school. However, a toddler was not an infrequent companion for some when in the field. So it happened that I was not immediately aware of Daisy's presence when they all climbed aboard my van at the appointed hour of collection one October Thursday morning during the 'sixties.

Later that same day, in the course of trying to sort out some grievance that Rue had failed to resolve, I chanced to look down the field and noticed two small yellow things, backed by a pink and white bulge, lying on the ground. Because of the distance it took me a few seconds to realise that it was one of the women. Thinking she must have fainted or been the victim of some quarrel, I set off at a fast pace to investigate. Passing one of the other pickers I motioned in the direction of my objective. The woman, alerted, stood up and turned to look: 'You don't want to worry about her. That's only Daisy. She's always fallin' over. It's them little feet of hers.'

I got a similar explanation from another woman further down the field. Not one of them seemed perturbed by their fellow picker's predicament. As I got closer I could see that the yellow things were a pair of Wellington boots. These were undoubtedly children's wear, for in those days adult Wellingtons were rarely in any other colour than black. The pink and white hump was, surprisingly, a white kitchen apron adorned with a loud rose design and tied to an exceedingly bulbous body form. On the opposite end of the tiny yellow boots was a small round face topped by a bright yellow waterproof storm cap, with white curls protruding below the turned up rim. The face beamed as I called, 'Are you okay?' 'Don't you worry, dear,' came the cheerful response. 'Just thought I'd measure the field.'

'It'll take you a long time to do it that way,' I advised, extending a hand to help her up and realising that Daisy was at least 70 years old, and most likely more. It was unusual to find a woman of her age in a potato field.

'You'll have to lift her by the shoulders,' called one of the other pickers working nearby, 'She have difficulty bending her knees.'

So I did as instructed. It was not an easy task to resurrect Daisy, who was surprisingly heavy, despite lack of height, but after a struggle I finally succeeded.

'Bless you dear, you're a real gentleman,' was her thanks.

It was then that I became fully aware of this extraordinary apparition; Daisy could not have been five feet in height, and she was the closest thing I have seen to someone being nearly as wide as they were tall. This apparent obesity was contained within a very threadbare but generous fawn raincoat, over the front of which was worn the aforementioned print apron. As far as I could see it was spotless, and I assumed she had forgotten to remove it before leaving home. The feet within the yellow boots must indeed have been tiny, the proportions which many a fashionable belle of her youth's generation would have considered a great asset. On a smooth pavement or path, no problem, but on rough ground they appeared quite insufficient to provide the necessary stability for the bulk above.

'Are you all right?' I queried. 'Had you been down there long?'

'Oh no dear, only about five minutes. I don't take no harm,' was her cheerful assurance.

'You'll catch your death of cold lying on that damp ground after the rain we had last night,' I scolded.

'Bless you dear, I won't take no harm. I got my rubber suit on and a leather jerkin under that. I could lie in a puddle all day and wouldn't take no harm.'

'Rubber suit?'

'Yes dear, one of them frogmen's suits the Navy used to use. My brother saw it in a government surplus store. Had to cut a fair bit off the arms and legs as them frogmen were a bit bigger than me. I'm well padded out underneath dear.'

I was astounded. 'It must get a bit hot in there on a day like this? I mean, it's not exactly cold,' I pondered out loud.

'Bless you dear, I don't move fast enough to really hot up. I only come 'tater pickin' for the company. Not worried if I don't fill many bags. And if I topple it gives me a rest. Only trouble I have is if I want to spend a penny. Wearin' this rubber suit it wouldn't do for me to be taken short.'

There was not time to elicit more information from Daisy, who seemed much too old for the back-straining task of potato picking. The tractor and trailer had arrived back in the field and Rue was calling for me to give Tim and him a hand lifting the full sacks on to the cart.

When I reached them Rue greeted me with, 'You can spend all day helpin' Daisy up if you've a mind. Best leave her be. The women'll do it when they get to her.'

'Can't she pick herself up?'

'Not if she fall on her back. She's just like an old sheep when it get on it's back. Lay there kickin' away but can't roll over. Tha's all that paddin' she wear that stop her, and them little old legs got no motion. Sometimes she's down for a quarter'n hour afore the women get to her. They keep an eye out for her though. Tha's why she wear them yellow boots and hat and that bright pinny. So she show up better when she's tumbled. Look like a bloody Donald Duck, don't she?'

Tim and I lifted another full sack on to the trailer and Rue placed it before continuing.

'You see how she do her pickin'? Bend from the waist and keep one hand on her pickin' pail to support herself. Don't have to bend her legs. Course, she can't bend 'em much with all that stuff she's got on.'

'How long has she been coming with the gang? I haven't noticed her before. She seems a bit old for the job. Is she hard up?' I asked.

'She's been here the last three days. Thought you'd have seen her. She come with the others in your van. She say she just come for the company and the other women like her. There she go again....'

We followed Rue's gaze, and sure enough the yellow boots were pointing skywards. Two women working nearby went to assist Daisy up, but at their first attempt they ended up on the ground with Daisy.

'There, look at that,' said Rue drily. 'When I was young I spent all my spare time tryin' to get girls on their backs. Now there's three doin' it for me and I'm too old to be interested.'

We ignored Rue's typical crude comment and watched as Daisy was hoisted upright.

'Tha's three times today already. Some days she go all day and never topple. Ground's rougher where she is today. Expect she caught her little old foot on a clod and over she went,' was Rue's further comment.

I did not see Daisy topple any more that day, but when the women had stopped for tea breaks and got into their usual huddle, occasional gusts of raucous laughter could be heard. If I am any judge I would say that it was dirty laughter. Intrigued, I asked Rue if he knew what all the frivolity were about. He shrugged his shoulders and said it only happened when Daisy was on the field. It was same thing the next day, Friday. A great deal of mirth issued from the gathering during the pickers' break for refreshment. When I came to pay the women I could not refrain from asking one of the more likeable among them, 'What was all that laughter about when you were having your lunch break?'

'That was Daisy. She have us in fits. You'd be surprised what she's done in her time, but I ain't tellin' you,' she laughed. I tried to obtain more details from one or two of the others but without success. When I came to pay Daisy, who had earned only a fraction of what any of the other pickers had, the temptation to ask about the hilarity was too great. 'You were certainly making the others laugh a lot Daisy. Were you telling them naughty stories?'

'Bless you dear, they'll laugh at anything. It were just woman's talk. Was telling them about some of the things I've seen in my time, helping to improve their education. I've always believed in a cheery word or two.'

No other details were revealed despite my further leading questions.

I went to get the van to return the gang to town. Arriving back at the field and helping them in, I looked around for Daisy. There she was, flat out on her back and giggling, having tripped in the headland furrow. I went to her aid. 'Just a'measuring your field again,' she beamed. One of the women helped me lift. 'That ain't the only thing she's measured in her time,' said the woman, a remark which set the others laughing.

On the following Monday I had business elsewhere and Tim fetched the women pickers. And that saw the last of the season's crop gathered in by lunchtime. We only grew potatoes for one more year and, as usual, only a few of the pickers who came had worked on our crop the previous year. Daisy was not among them, but I was told she was still around.

I never set eyes on her again, and know no more about her than is related here. The unknown always fascinates and I have often thought of that strange orb-like figure in the yellow boots and storm hat and wondered just what made her so entertaining to those women half her age. Daisy is probably measuring some churchyard now. I can't say I'm tormented by women, more like mystified, but I can sometimes see what Rue meant.

The Village Idiot

VILLAGE idiots are not a myth; they were very obvious in this district when I was a lad. Just about every village had one, if not more, and they were, with few exceptions, male. Their mental derangement varied greatly, as did the local terminology for their condition – dafters, nutters, loons and so on.

They were all harmless; well, those of my acquaintance, and from the poorer families. The usual assertion for their being what they were was that it was down to inbreeding. It is true that until the early part of this century this was common in country communities, where the long working days left little time for going in search of a mate. Cousins, aunts and uncles intermarrying was not uncommon.

Be that as it may, perhaps the gentry produced just as many nutters but kept them out of sight. The working class families had no option but to find their idiots some work they could cope with or just let them wander free. The asylums of the time were reserved for the unmanageable.

Our village had two notable nutters who were often to be seen wandering the roads or tottering about in the village street. There was a general acceptance that such individuals existed in rural society and that they were neither pitied nor maligned by villagers. Only those residents who were comparative newcomers to the village would cross to the other side of the road if confronted by a halfwit, simply because they felt ill at ease in their presence. Not so true country folk. They thought no more of exchanging a few words with a loony than any other local who might be encountered. In the last decades of the twentieth century you will be unlikely to find any loonies wandering the villages. They have all been closeted as the rural scene has become sanitized. Mental institutions now subject these individuals to therapeutic and neuropathic courses at the taxpayer's expense, while I dare say the subjects would be far happier walking free as they did in years gone by.

Yes, those of my memory were happy souls, if one can trust outward signs. I suspect most of the loonies I knew looked on the rest of us as being the stupid ones. Both our village nutters had a periodic urge to exercise their vocal chords. The most evident was Treacle, who wandered about the village street shouting and gesticulating at traffic, his favourite being the big red double-decker bus. What he shouted was incomprehensible, or at best gibberish, so that when hailed, many a car driver who was a stranger in these parts, thinking some vital information had been given would make an emergency stop, reverse and politely ask what the problem was, only to be greeted with a grin and, 'I weren't talking to you.'

Treacle was a man about as old as the century and usually clad in a pinstripe suit that one of the gentlemen his mother charred for had passed on. About the only employment ever bestowed on Treacle was bird scaring. The problem was that he quickly tired of ambling around the field he had been put to protect from rooks and pigeons and pursued his occasional rantings against other creatures in the neighbourhood. Unfortunately this included the dairy herd of the farmer who had employed him. Cows rudely disturbed from their grazing go off their milk, so the farmer dispensed with Treacle's services, not that Treacle cared; he was much happier in the street raving at the Eastern Counties bus.

Grimble was a little younger than Treacle and one of a large family. His mother explained Grimble's permanent grin, occasional stuttered word, and uncontrolled habit of letting out high-pitched screeches when excited, to his having had "sleeping sickness" when he was an infant. The name Grimble was derived from his continual picking of his nose whilst shambling about the village street, where he would often follow Treacle. Grimble was more gregarious and

would surely join any gossip gathering outside The Wheelwright's Arms, where he would be accepted but ignored. The locals had long ago given up telling him to "bugger off" as Grimble took no notice.

There were times when Grimble's liking for company did cause a few problems; such as the post-natal clinic at the doctor's surgery where he was disinclined to leave unless his demand to be examined was met. Then there was the coachload of bible thumpers from London on a day out trip to spread the word to the infidels in rural parts. On the way back to London they thought the screeches that periodically issued from one of their number was just religious fervour. They had reached Romford before they realised that Grimble was not one of their flock.

Over the years the unprincipled exploited Treacle and Grimble in various pranks to worry strangers; Treacle and Grimble always being willing, if unknowingly co-operative. One unscrupulous political activist conceived an idea to heckle the Labour candidate at the 1950 General Election. He persuaded Treacle and Grimble to accompany him to the meeting through the sacrifice of his confectionery ration: a piece of chocolate as bait and a bit more once seated in the village hall. Treacle was encouraged to make one of his shouting and arm-waving displays, at which the instigator persuaded some of his cronies to applaud.

The poor parliamentary candidate was certainly taken aback, particularly as the outburst came during an uncontentious part of his speech. The applause must have inspired Treacle to give a repeat performance. The Chairman, sensing a Tory plot, told Treacle to sit down and shut up. More applause and the beaming Treacle gave yet another display. The Chairman again tried to restore order, but his words were partly drowned by one of Grimble's excited screeches.

The meeting degenerated into chaos as local Labour supporters tried to eject Treacle and Grimble. Events developed far beyond the instigator's expectations, but his smug delight was soon shattered. The two loonies so enjoyed the experience they needed little encouragement from a few Labourites to become just as vocal when the Conservative candidate spoke a few nights later. There followed claims and counter claims of unethical behaviour in the heated exchanges between the two camps. Treacle and Grimble were oblivious to all this fuss, while the majority of unaligned villagers thought it a great joke.

The most notorious loony in this district was Joey Two Beans. His major problem was forgetfulness, apart from the fact that, like Grimble, he rarely uttered more than a single word at a time, which was invariably accompanied by a few giggles. The origin of his strange if intriguing nickname is unknown to me. I recall him as a tall, gangling fellow with a permanent grin. Joey Two Beans frequented the streets of a little market town a few miles north-west of our village.

Each morning his mother would dress him and turn him out to wander while she went off to work. Joey would shuffle harmlessly around the pavements, occasionally stopping to watch the world go by and to acknowledge salutations with a gurgled 'morning.' Unfortunately, Joey's forgetfulness was most evident when he had visited the gentlemen's convenience just off the High Street. For not only was he disinclined to do up buttons, he frequently failed to tuck away that part of his anatomy he had removed. The townspeople had long grown used to Joey Two Beans' forgetfulness, and while it might be an exaggeration to say no one raised an eyelid, his failing was accepted with no more recourse than to remind him sharply to "put it away Joey." Sadly, Joey's mental state was such that any orders made to him frequently had no effect. As a result, down-to-earth women of the town did not hesitate to do the task for him and button him up. Even the District Nurse thought this a sensible course of action, but she always put on gloves.

There were those in the community who suggested that Joey was not as daft as he appeared and was deliberately playing dumb in this matter. The women who thought no more of tidying Joey up than washing their front doorsteps were well known, and the less dutiful and more bashful matrons would carry the word down the street to them. 'Joey Two Beans is showing again Mavis.' And Mavis, Brenda, Bessie or anyone of these guardians of the town's propriety would make haste to the scene.

Joey Two Beans shuffled around the town for years with little public fuss at his occasional lapses. Eventually the spread of urbanisation began to touch even this Suffolk rural backwater; everyman's motor car began to remove the remoteness. New commuter homes sprang up and ushered in the Yuppie era. The newcomers brought their ideas of morality and social conduct with them and expected those they had come amongst to conform to these. Self interest ruled supreme.

So it was that one day in the early 'seventies the wife of a young executive parked her Volvo Estate in the High Street, took her four-year-old daughter by the hand and headed for the little greengrocer's shop on the corner of School Lane. As she was about to enter, the small girl observed, 'Mummy, that man's got a thing like Daddy.' The woman turned to look, saw and almost dragged the child into the shop, such was her acceleration to escape the scene. The child, as children always do, had to enlarge on the subject. 'It's bigger than Daddy's.'

Even the Estee Lauder facial could not hide the executive wife's flush as she gasped at the greengrocer lady, 'There's a man out there who has just exposed himself to me.' The greengrocer lady looked out of the window and reassuringly observed, 'No need to worry dear, that's only Joey Two Beans. He's not quite the ticket. Just forgets. Don't mean no harm. Most times someone has to do it for him.'

As she spoke she walked towards the entrance. 'I'll be back in a minute. Shan't be a jiffy.' And as children are apt to do, the small girl kept going on about what she had just seen. 'Why did that man ....' The mother cut her short, scolding, 'I don't want to hear any more about it.'

'Why?'

'Because it is not nice. The man should be locked up.'

'Why?'

The flustered woman received some relief from this questioning by the return of the greengrocer lady. 'That's that. Now what can I get you?'

The executive's wife stood aghast; 'Aren't you going to wash your hands before you serve me?'

The greengrocer lady chuckled. 'Oh I didn't do it. I just went next door and told Mrs Brown. She's always tidying Joey.'

The matter did not rest there. The executive wife complained to her husband and he went to the local police, who were no more troubled by Joey Two Beans than the rest of the old community. The executive wife and her husband mustered the powerful influence of other executive wives and husbands, plus the local gentry who had in the past "passed by" on the other side of the road. The town council was approached: Joey Two Beans must be removed to a mental institution.

There was considerable opposition from the oldies, who did not take to being bossed about by the newies. Eventually someone suggested a brilliant compromise. Joey Two Beans should be made to wear a short but heavy apron. Any lapses in buttoning would then be automatically attended to. This worked like a charm. Every morning Joey's mother would tie on the apron securely and Joey was able to wander the streets without causing offence to anyone.

That is, until the opening of the little town's first supermarket. On that day an actress of national standing was imported by the supermarket company to cut the ceremonial ribbon and open the store. There was a howling gale blowing right down the High Street but this did not deter a fair-sized crowd from gathering. The actress cut the ribbon and thereafter forgot her lines as a result of glancing across the street where the strong wind was lifting Joey Two Beans' apron. The crowd, seeing the actress had lost her composure, turned to see what was the cause, just as an extra strong gust of wind lifted...well, a description is unnecessary.

Suffice to say that a few weeks later Joey Two Beans was placed in a home, where the State paid nurses to keep him tidy until his dying day. Joey Two Beans' confinement was the price of the new society's prudery. The Joey Two Beans, Treacles, Grimbles and the rest have long been swept from our scene. Village life was richer when they were around.

The Shadow Men

ONE OF THE very noticeable changes in our countryside during the past half-century has been human attention. In the earlier years it was foremost a provider – beyond the normal uses of agriculture. Hedgerows and woodlands were sources of food and fuel. Rabbits and pigeons for the pot, blackberries and bullaces for the pie, mushrooms and moorhens eggs, hazelnuts and elderberries and much, much more. No branch or tree fell without it being quickly sawn and chopped for the home fire. Footpaths were short cuts to places of intemperance or places of worship.

Nowadays surviving hedgerows and woodland remain comparatively untroubled by man, as does the wildlife therein. The footpaths are used by those who walk for pleasure and exercise, but mostly by dog owners who prefer their pets to mess on someone else's property rather than their own. In short, the urban fugitives who predominate in the village see the countryside as a place in which to live, not a place to live off. The late twentieth century Englishman pays homage to the trinity of motor car, supermarket and television; the provisions of nature have become incidentals.

There is no comfortable alternative to accepting change. Even so, there remains a wistfulness for many aspects of the departed scene; people and practices, the sights and sayings of particular times. For example, when did I last hear anyone talk of Shadow Men? Not for a quarter of a century, at least, for I doubt if there have been Shadow Men around here since the 'sixties. Shadow Men was the generic term for those individuals whose activities were never out in the open, sometimes clandestine, but not necessarily so. More a case that the individuals concerned were loners. I once heard Rue respond to a landgirl's question as to what was meant by Shadow Men by saying that they were men who were out and about when most others were still in bed.

Briar Smith was most certainly a Shadow Man. That is old Briar Smith; his son goes by the same nickname although it is now just a hand-me-down. The son is a storeman at Tesco's and has never had anything to do with the business that earned his father this epithet. There was once a worthwhile job in providing briar stocks for the grafting of garden roses; the hedges and woodlands were a ready source of the dog roses from which these stocks were taken.

Few farmers or landowners would have objected to anyone taking these stocks providing gaps were not made in hedges, yet as far as I know, Briar Smith never approached anyone for permission. Instead, he would be about at first light when the fields and woods were silent, taking here and taking there in a way that left little evidence of his acquisitions. Few people ever claim to have seen him at work, for Briar Smith had both the cunning and the hearing of a fox. Should anyone else come his way at daybreak he would disappear from view, concealed behind a convenient bush or tree, until the passer-by was gone. Any such person was likely to be another Shadow Man for, as has been said, most folk were still asleep.

Those of us who knew the signs could sometimes find where Briar Smith had been. The stock was usually a runner from an established dog rose bush in the hedgerow. Where the soil had been disturbed in digging the root, a covering of fallen leaves, twigs or some other camouflage was applied to conceal the taking. This was hard to spot, but briars pruned from the stock were usually the giveaway. For while Briar Smith would tuck these neatly up and hopefully out of sight in the mass of the main bush, in time the dead pruning would turn from green to brown and was more easily seen. However, the uninitiated would never know a Shadow Man had passed that way.

To whom Briar Smith sold his takings I know not. Nor do I know if it were a profitable undertaking. These matters were shrouded in secrecy like the rest of his activities. But he has been departed from this life many years now and the dog roses grow and spread undisturbed. A jolly man, and willing to mardle unless one mentioned his trade, whereupon he would claim such was all gossip and untrue, plus a reminder that as a jobbing gardener he had no need of other income. Interestingly, unlike almost every other garden in the village, there was not a single rose in Briar Smith's garden. He professed he didn't like them.

The Shadow Man that I knew best was Billy Fogget. His activities were more public although he, like Briar, preferred to work when the eastern sky began to lighten. A bachelor, Billy had become an anachronism by the mid twentieth century. His small thatched cottage was lit by an oil lamp, heated by a wood-fuelled stove and watered from a well. Motor cars may have raced along on the nearby road and aircraft soared in the sky above, but Billy's cottage remained much as it must have been in Victorian times. No tradesmen called, no newspaper was delivered, and I doubt that the postman made many visits. Billy collected his bread and what else he required from the village store, albeit his purchases were meagre. Apart from a few annuals that brightened the edges of the path to his front door, his garden was set with fruit and vegetables that marked his near self-sufficiency. Beyond his hen run a collection of small sheds had padlocked doors but the scent of rabbit and ferret that permeated the surrounding area gave fair indication of what was housed therein.

As for Billy Fogget himself, he remains in memory as a weasel face beneath a cloth cap and above a heavy overcoat. The shoulders seemed ever hunched and the face downturned, perhaps the result of always looking at the ground, for there he plied his trade. Billy Fogget was a mole catcher. He also dealt with vermin and took other wild creatures, but his principal preoccupation was with moles. If one had a problem with these miners word was sent via the landlord of The Anchor for Fogget to come.

Billy Fogget was a man of similar disposition to Charlie Gaybarrow, the grave digger, and many others of that same generation who seemed to prefer their own individual company. Fogget rarely drank with others and went for his weekly pint as soon as the pub opened in the evening. He would be gone before the regulars began to roll in around seven.

Another reason for Billy's early visit was his philosophy as once expressed to me as, 'The Good Lord made darkness so as man could sleep, and daylight so as man would be up and about. I don't hold with sitting up with a lamp; tha's against nature. When the nights is long a man needs more sleep to fortify him against the winter weather. In summer when tha's warmer he don't need to be abed so long.'

And Billy practised what he preached. One could bang on his door after dark but he would never answer. And, apart from Sundays, he was rarely to be found at home during the day. Yet his garden was always tidy, bountiful and never a weed to be seen. So if one had mole trouble and wanted to employ Billy's services the procedure was either a message left at The Anchor or a note pushed under Billy's door.

Over the years we occasionally had cause to send for Billy when too many moles invaded the cow pastures. We could have put down a few traps ourselves, except that our success was always minimal, and Billy always restored order quickly and without fail. When he had received a message to call he would arrive in the farmyard around midday, a time which he appeared to reserve for what he considered the unproductive hours; 'Ain't no good thinkin' you're goin' to catch moles when the sun is high.' Billy would then inspect the site of the disruption and eye up the molehills; he always spent several minutes doing this.

Then, when he had his fill he would invariably announce, 'Will be done tomorrow morning,' and departed. Tomorrow morning for Billy would be long before the still-yawning Clive set forth to scatter the dew at 5.30 and drive the cows in to milk. I never saw Billy at work, nor do I know how he did his job; only that no more molehills appeared in the troubled pasture that season.

It would be a few days before Billy would appear in the farmyard again and ask, 'Them moles gone?' This was really a request for payment. He never set a price. While I knew Billy had a contact who collected and paid for moleskins, I always rewarded him generously for his expertise.

On one such occasion when he was obviously mellowed by my handout I tried to learn something of the methods he used to catch moles. This brought a mild rebuff, 'If I was to tell people what I does I'd be doin' meself out of a job.' I sympathised and suggested this was one of the reasons he did his work when no one else was about to see his methods. This he denied, repeating his view that a man should be risen as soon as it was daylight. Even so, I think I was right in my surmise.

Another time when we were talking I noticed a movement in his coat pocket and mentioned this. Billy put his hand in the pocket and, to my astonishment, withdrew a weasel, a "mousehunt" he said, before returning the animal from whence it had come. I enquired if it had just been caught, and wouldn't it escape? 'Tha's tame. I got a pair. They're no trouble.' My further questions as to why he carried one in his pocket brought a half grin to that weasel countenance and another rebuff, 'I'm not saying.' "Mousehunt" is a local Suffolk name for a weasel. I doubt that Billy kept them for hunting mice.

In his later years much of Billy Fogget's mole catching activities were performed on the garden lawns of the middle class newcomers to the village. Notice of such work was occasionally channelled through me, such as when Mrs Ludington-Witt asked if I knew how to rid her garden of a plague of moles. A note slipped under Fogget's cottage door read, 'Mrs Ludington-Witt at Oak House has 15 molehills on her lawn. She would like you to get rid of the moles.'

A couple of weeks later Billy called about another matter and I casually asked how he had got on with Mrs Ludington-Witt. A tender nerve had been touched; 'Her! I spent two mornin's there and cleared them right out. And do you know what she gave me? "Well done my man" she says, "here's a half a crown". A half a crown!' There is none meaner than the well-to-do – and the Ludington-Witts were not short of a penny.

A fortnight on and there was another telephone call from Mrs Ludington-Witt. Could I arrange for the mole catcher to call again. He had rid her lawn of them completely after his visit but suddenly there were twice as many as before. I had passed the message to Fogget even though I could not see him going again. There were other frantic appeals from Mrs Ludington-Witt that autumn but Billy Fogget never went back, well, not to catch moles. It must have been the following year during one of our brief conversations that I again remarked about Mrs Ludington-Witt. I thought I saw a trace of a grin on that weasel face as he snapped, 'I can give 'em as well as take 'em.'

Billy Fogget is another of the "owd boys" who is long gone. I can understand his reluctance to divulge the tricks of his trade for fear that he might have a competitor, although I doubt if it would have been easy for a newcomer to match his skills. What is sad is that all his knowledge died with him and is lost. There is only speculation as to how he caught moles or kept them away, or his equal expertise of ridding a barn of vermin. And I can only guess at the use to which the mousehunts were put.

When Billy died it is said all manner of animal furs were found hung up to dry in one of his sheds, including a number of stoat tails. The sheds have long gone too. In their place stands a double garage for a commuter's cars. The cottage thatch has given way to the same modern red tile that is on the extension, which is almost as large as the original dwelling. The exterior walls between the modern double glazed windows are rose pink and the front door a trendy gloss black finish.

Old Billy would hardly recognize the place. Perhaps he would approve of one piece of recognition of the past that the new owner has bestowed. The wording on the rather twee nameplate reads: "Molecatcher's Cottage".

As Tight as . . .

A PERIOD of dry weather was broken by a thunder storm and it was necessary to get out my rubber boots to walk across the meadows. Unfortunately, I had forgotten that earlier in the year one boot had developed a crack, and after only a few yards in the sward my left foot felt decidedly wet. By the time I had reached the gate into Friar's Lane the leaking boot squelched with every step.

Threading my way between the still-dripping overhanging hedges towards that part of the lane which broadens into a wide track, I caught sight of the familiar shape of old Newson up ahead, out for an evening stroll with that whining bull terrier of his. Happening to look over his shoulder and seeing me, he stopped until I caught up. Obviously a mardle was in the offing.

'Evenin' young master,' a familiar salutation which always made me wince as both categories were false.

'Hello Mr Newson.'

'What you hobblin' along like that for? Ain't forgot yourself have you?'

'I've got a wet foot. Hole in my rubber boot.'

'Time you bought yourself a new pair then. They's cheap enough nowadays. Two tight I suspect, like all you old farmers,' he parried with a grin.

'It's not that. I just haven't had a chance to get another pair,' I countered, irked by this assertion of frugality.

'Ah, there's never so tight as a farmer. Won't part with a penny until they's forced.' He had a point, but I wasn't going to encourage him. We still had a quarter of a mile to go before the end of the lane and it was bad enough having to reduce my pace to walk with him without suffering a diatribe on the failings of my profession. But, of course, he was just looking for an excuse to exercise his wealth of anecdotes.

'Meanest man I ever knew were a farmer. Isaac Brown what had that little pightle farm just off the Ipswich road at Holton. He were cousin of Herbert Brown, that little owd fellow my cousin Aggie took for her second, before him she were married to Wrightway what had the first set of falsies round here. One of them Browns is related to your Rue Scrutts by marriage. I ain't sure but I think tha's Herbert's sister. Yes, that can't have been Isaac Brown's sister 'cause he were an only. There's Browns at Horkesley but they ain't no relation, and I hear there's a fellow of that name just moved into old Soddin' Sykes' house. But he's one of them Yippies.'

I didn't bother to correct old Newson, who often had trouble getting the right word, as I was more intent on diverting him from this long and involved survey of whom was related to who. 'What about this mean farmer?'

'Hold you back a bit, then I'll tell you. You're walkin' too fast for me. Stands to reason he'd be mean 'cause his mother were a Jewish girl and them Browns come down from Scotland originally. He ought to have been called MacBrownstein. Meanness in the blood.'

'That's a bit unfair, isn't it?' My effort at moderation was smartly rejected; 'You ask anybody that knowed him. Tight as a duck's arse, and you know how tight that is, don't you? Tha's watertight!' I managed a weak smile at his hackneyed crudity, although old Newson did not wait for appreciative response, having really got to grips with his tale.

'Isaac Brown were an old bachelor and they's always the worst. Someone once asked him if he'd ever thought about gettin' a wife. Brown said he couldn't spare time for thinkin'. He weren't civil to no one; but you don't have to worry that he might spit on you. He weren't goin' to give anything away free.' There was a short pause as old Newson dabbed at his mouth with a spotted handkerchief;

always a curiosity, no one else has spotted handkerchiefs these days.

'That little owd farm were derelict before Brown took it, just a mass of weeds in the meadows. I'll give him his due, he soon got that round. One day the owd vicar come and asked Brown for somethin' to put in the church for Harvest Festival. The vicar say, "The Good Lord have worked wonders in your fields and provided you with bountiful crops." Brown say, "Pity the Lord didn't take the opportunity to provide bountiful crops when he had the fields all to himself", and shut the door. Did ever you hear the likes of that?'

'One of those women that collect for charity went to Brown's door once and asked him to put something in her can. He spun her such a tale of woe that he couldn't afford to live and couldn't afford to die that she gave him all the money she'd already collected. Do you know, he sewed up his pockets so he couldn't put any money in, and like that he wouldn't be able to take any out. He didn't waste anything. He made the leaves in his teapot last a week and the water he washed in he'd use for his dishes and then give it to his pigs 'cause he reckoned that it picked up some goodness on the way. If he heard anything were goin' free he'd be there. Never bought a glass of beer, said that was a waste of money. But when the brewery had to get rid of some ale they didn't think would keep they offered full barrels free to them that would collect 'em. Brown took a couple and drank the lot in a week. Took up beer drinkin' on Monday and gave up on Friday when he'd finished the last barrel – reckon he were twice as tight as usual that week, if you get my meaning. Never touched a drop after that as far as I know. Said he wouldn't drink again 'til he could find something cheaper than what he'd already had.'

'And talkin' about drinkin', one hot summer day a traveller stopped at Brown's farm and asked if he could have a glass of water from the well. Brown say, "That'll cost you sixpence". The fellow asked why as the well water didn't cost Brown nothing. Brown told him he was forgetting the wear and tear on his bucket and glass and the time he'd spent emptying and filling. Did ever you hear such a thing?

'No one would work for him because he wouldn't pay proper

wages. There was a one-armed man who went to him for a job. Brown told him he can have a job but as he'd only got one arm he reckoned he'd only be able to do half the job so he was only going to pay him half the pay. The one-armed fellow told him he could keep his job and said that he was half a mind to report him. Brown said that had he have known before that the fellow had only half a mind he'd have cut the pay to a quarter.'

The squelching of my foot in the waterlogged wellington prompted old Newson to divert from his tale and warn, 'If you don't hurry home and get out of that wet boot you'll get duck foot disease.' Having no intention of being regaled with the horrors of duck foot disease, whatever it entailed, I ignored the comment. 'Yes, I'll certainly have to get rid of this. I never knew the hole was so large.'

'I bet there ain't no holes in your pockets. Don't know a farmer with money in his pocket that would let it escape easy. Here, don't like to see a fellow suffering. Take this tenpenny piece towards buying a new pair of wellies.' He held out his hand.

Of course, he was only teasing, but I got a new pair of Wellingtons first thing next day. There is nothing like a veiled accusation of meanness, even in jest, to spur one to benevolence. Well, if helping to fill the shopkeeper's till counts as benevolence.

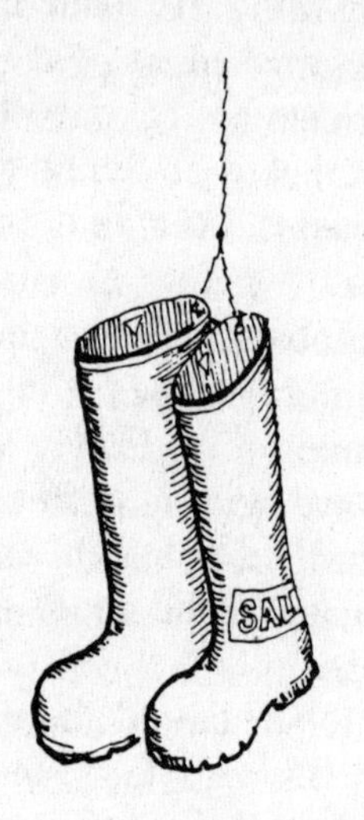

Some time I must ask old Newson what happened to Isaac Brown. He must have scrooged a few pounds away. If he were as mean as Harry Newson makes out then he was unlikely to leave it to anyone. And he couldn't have taken it with him – or could he?

What a Wedding!

'MY GRANDDAUGHTER is going to get churched next month and I'd like you to come to the service and the reception.'

Weddings outside the family are not really my scene. But I have always liked Archie, who worked for us for more than thirty years before retiring, so the invitation was accepted providing the date did not clash with anything else already fixed.

'February isn't the month for a wedding. Would have thought she would wait until the spring,' I posed.

'That'd be too late then. She's six months gone. Can't wait, these youngsters nowadays. Mind you, I can quite understand it. If the Good Lord had anything better he must have kept it to himself.' This philosophical view was delivered in Archie's usual matter-of-fact way; he might just as easily have been discussing his vegetable garden. A chuckle seemed appropriate even if no indication had been given as to whether he, personally, viewed his granddaughter's condition favourably or otherwise. From following comments he was obviously only concerned with the practicalities of the situation.

'My daughter has got a problem because she want the gal to wear the white wedding dress that she got married in. Only that has got to be let out in the front and she can't do it until nearer the wedding day because she don't know how big the gal will be. She's already showing like that's going to be twins.'

'Tricky,' was my adjudged, diplomatic observation. My thoughts were otherwise.

A formal invitation, all hearts and cherubs, was received through the post a few days later. The date was free in my calendar, but my wife was less inclined to participate in the jollities and made some excuse for declining. A suitable present was obtained and sent with my formal acceptance. I knew Archie's daughter but had not set eyes on her family since they were toddlers, not to know who they were, that is.

On the Saturday of the wedding my intention was to go to the church and make only a brief appearance at the reception in the village hall. At ten to two the church was already fairly full and humming with the chatter and excitement of children. I selected a pew at the back and sat down beside old Bramble Blake, who had on a dark grey suit. The suit was a bit short in the sleeve and leg and probably nearly as old as I am; the smell of camphor suggested several decades of exposure to mothballs. After exchanging nods, Bramble Blake leaned over and said, 'Didn't know he were so popular.'

'I didn't know him either. Archie asked me to come,' I responded.

'Archie? Thought he couldn't stand the sight of him. I shouldn't say it but I never knew a more miserable so-and-so. He'll depress them in Heaven if he's lucky enough to get there. I wouldn't be here if I weren't related.'

The realisation that Bramble could not be referring to the bridegroom prompted me to ask who he was talking about.

'Why Arthur Sparrow. Him they called Porky. It's his funeral ain't it? Two o' clock.'

Pulling out my crumpled invitation and passing it to Bramble Blake brought an insistence that he had definitely been given the same time for the funeral. The vicar had been known to get his dates muddled before, and as he was now happily chatting to the groom and best man he must still have been blissfully unaware of this mix-up.

The next thought was that someone should tell somebody while there was still time to avert an embarrassing situation. There was not time. Either the undertaker's watch was fast or he was eager to get the job done, for at that moment the coffin and bearers entered the church. There was a pronounced hush as the coffin was drawn up the aisle.

From the looks on the bearers' faces they were surprised to see such a gathering. Nowhere near so surprised as the vicar or bridegroom and best man when the coffin arrived beside them. There was a stunned silence in the front row. The bride's mother went weak at the knees and the best man dropped the ring. While the ring was retrieved someone, unknown to me, ran from the church to try and halt the bridal car before it reached the church. He was successful because, as almost always, the bride was late. After a brief consultation with the vicar the best man turned and addressed the congregation: 'There's been a bit of a...mess-up and the vicar say's he's sorry. But if you together will hang on he'll get Mr Sparrow done first as he can't leave him lying about while he see to us.'

One had to hand it to the best man for sorting things out. The vicar appeared to be taking longer to regain his composure, and from his restatement of what had just been announced, using more appropriate language, the signs were that he did not like the best man usurping his authority.

And so it came to pass that little Arthur Sparrow was sent on his way with what must have been the biggest gathering for a funeral service that that church had seen for many a year. Probably the speediest funeral too, the bearers nearly breaking into a trot when they whisked the coffin out to the churchyard.

As soon as the vicar returned and gave the okay, the best man went to tell the bride she could now make her entrance.

'Well, now I'm here I might as well make the most of it and stay for the next one. Doubt I'll be here again until they carry me in like they just done old Sparrow,' Bramble Blake observed from his perch beside me. And as the bride appeared and padded up the aisle he further remarked, dryly, 'Heard she was marrying a petrol pump attendant. Looks like he's already filled her tank with four-star.'

Unwisely, whoever it was who had checked the bride's arrival had diverted her, her father and the bridesmaids into the warmth of The Wheelwright's Arms. There, the landlord, who certainly had cause to mark this as a unique occasion, was generous with a bottle of brandy. As a result, during the service the bride kept giggling and turning to look at the bridesmaids, who could not refrain from tittering. There can be nothing more irritating to a vicar trying to conduct a serious ceremony than to have four tittering maids and a giggling bride.

At one point he lost his place and started to read part of the christening service until the organist tiptoed across and whispered in his ear. I do not, however, believe his words were, as later circulated on the village gossip roundabout, 'You're about three months too early with that one, Vicar.'

The nuptials finally completed, the knot safely tied, the precocious best man took it upon himself to stand up and announce, 'Them what's come for Mr Sparrow is very welcome to come to the reception if they have a mind.' At a guess most of those who had gone to the funeral finished up at the wedding breakfast, although a rural rave-up would be a more apt description. I might have enjoyed it more if Archie hadn't buttonholed me as soon as I entered the hall door and placed me at a table beside his elder sister whom he wanted me to meet.

'This is my sister Annie what have come from Lowestoft. Annie, this is Mr Freeman who I used to work for.' And then, turning back to me, 'You'd never believe she's 79 would you? Just a bit hard of hearing but apart from that she's as fit as a fiddle.'

Indeed this lady did not appear near 80 either in looks (no doubt helped by her hair being dyed ginger) or agility. I was quickly made aware that her hearing was not up to much by her opening remark, albeit there was a considerable din in the hall. 'When he said you'd been freed do he mean you been to prison?' I explained that was not what Archie had said and a young woman sitting opposite also endeavoured to put the old lady right.

'This is my grand niece, Betty. Archie's daughter's youngest. She ain't been stuffing herself with Mars bars like her sister.'

The girl opposite gave me a knowing grin; evidently the bride's great aunt Annie had not been informed on certain matters and I was not going to enlighten her, although I am sure she knew the situation well enough. At this point the best man, apparently the self-appointed master of ceremonies, asked if we would get up and help slide the tables a little further down the hall so the bride could sit down. The top table had been backed so far up against the stage there was insufficient room for her to squeeze into her seat.

Great aunt Annie revealed an obstinate streak in refusing to get up from her chair and as a result of the reshuffle our table was separated from the rest. There were four places; that beside the grand niece was empty, kept for her boyfriend who was to arrive later. Also as a result of the rearrangement I was now seated on the opposite side of Aunt Annie. 'What are you doing that side?' she scolded, 'I wish you wouldn't keep movin' about. Or are you deaf in the right ear?' The girl opposite obligingly explained why I had been forced to change seat positions. To which Annie felt a need to repeat, 'That's my grand niece, Betty. She lives at Longham. Where do you live?'

'Auntie is a bit absentminded. Hope you'll forgive her,' interjected the young woman as I was about to reply.

'Don't you be so cheeky, young Betty. If he don't tell me where he lives how am I to know?' And then, turning to me, 'Do you live in the same place as you did before you went to prison?' It was fast dawning that the conversation with this elderly matron would be difficult. Thus I was relieved when the Master of Ceremonies announced, 'You can get stuck in together,' which was rural Suffolk for getting eating and drinking.

Great Aunt Annie proved to be a pernickety eater, declining most of the fare offered her until she set her eyes on a bowl of pickled onions.

'Nothing I like better than pickled onions. My daughter who I live with at Lowestoft she won't have them, just because they wham a bit.' With that she tipped out about a half dozen pickles from the bowl and proceeded to eat them, using finger and thumb to place them in her mouth. Her table manners one could forgive, the loud chomping that ensued was a different matter, particularly as now and then small pieces of masticated pickled onion escaped from her mouth. My smoked salmon, thus decorated, I declined to finish. Pity; it had been quite tasty. In order, hopefully, to put a stop to this enforced proximity to pickled onion munching I volunteered, 'They are very indigestible, you know. Are you sure you should eat all those?'

'They do you good, not harm. So long as you don't drink alcohol at the same time you're all right. That's when people swill a lot of beer while they're eating pickled onions that you get trouble – they can be proper upsetting then. Before I married and moved away there was an old fellow round here called Draughty Dodds. That's what he was always doin', he'd get through two or three pints of stout and a half jar of pickled onions inside him and you should have heard his old guts. A'rumblin' around like a volcano about to erupt – and that did – often.'

'Auntie!' scolded the girl opposite.

'Yes, I've heard about Draughty Dodds. Would you like me to pour you a drink of water?' Better to divert the lady to some other thought; we were on dangerous grounds if all I had heard about Draughty Dodds was true. No reply was forthcoming, only some more slopping noises. Great Aunt Annie's jaws and mouth were going through a series of contortions. Finally she opened her mouth, stuck in her right index finger and appeared to be levering at something. The next thing Annie had removed her false teeth and set them on the table. 'There. That's the cause of the trouble,' she slobbered, 'Couldn't shift it with my finger.' A large piece of pickled onion was wedged at the back between top and bottom plates.

'Really Gran. That isn't a very nice thing to do in front of everybody.' Her grand niece was clearly embarrassed.

'What do you expect me to do girl? Sit there unable to say another word to this gentleman all evening?' Then, turning to me, 'Would you be so kind as to pull that lump out. My hands are none too steady nowadays.'

'You can't ask him to do that. Here, let me.' The horrified girl took a napkin and gripped the gnashers and waggled the piece of onion loose. One could tell it was not a task she relished. The teeth returned from whence they had come and I repeated my question about a glass of water.

'Tea. I'd love a good cup of tea,' Great Aunt Annie demanded. Tea was sent for. When it came the ageing matron proceeded to pour it from the cup into the saucer. 'That cool better this way,' and then lifted the saucer to her lips. The following noise as the tea was more sucked than sipped was worse than the pickled onion chomping. At least there was no fallout. The grand niece looked at me and winced, 'I think she does this on purpose just to stir it up.'

The saucer was removed from the mouth and we were told, 'I don't take sugar so there's no need for me to stir it up.' Even I was beginning to think the old girl was not as hard of hearing as she made out. However, her attention now turned to the two hairy young men in bomber jackets and very tight jeans who had appeared carrying an assortment of cases and equipment. 'Who are these, more from the funeral?'

'No Auntie, they're the disco come to play,' the girl obliged.

'We don't want that row. Won't be able to hear yourself speak. I wouldn't have come if I'd have known. Ridiculous in a little hall like this.'

In my opinion this was the most sense Great Aunt Annie had spoken since my first making her acquaintance. By the look of the many large speakers being erected the noise would be deafening. Now was the time to excuse myself and leave. Before I could tell Annie and her grand niece of my impending departure, the prospective geriatric started to shuffle her chair away from the table. 'I'm goin' to the Ladies and if that row that passes for music is as bad as I expect I shall lock the door and stay there,' she threatened as she stood up. The girl looked alarmed, 'You can't do that. There's only one loo in the building.' Annie ignored the plea, leaned across the table and picked up a full jug of water.

'What do you want that for?' the girl asked.

'I know these village hall toilets. The flush probably won't work so I'm takin' this.' And off she went.

After a brief goodbye to the grand niece, I thanked Archie and his daughter and wished the newlyweds well. The bride was still giggling and tittering and the groom wasn't much better, having imbibed far too freely. As for the cocky best man, he had reached the status of the proverbial coot. No doubt all present were having a very good time, including those who had originally set out to mourn.

As I was about to go through the hall entrance there was a very loud 'wham' from somewhere in the back. The lights flickered and all the disco lights went out completely. The disco boys were tuning up or whatever it is they do to make that infernal din and this also stopped abruptly. The hall's three plug electrical system had obviously failed. At least those who didn't like discos would get relief until the fuses were mended.

***

A few days later Archie dropped by the farm. 'Hope you didn't mind me putting you with Annie. I thought you'd be able to keep her in check. She will play up at gatherings, always did.'

'Yes, I did think she was not as deaf or as daft as she made out.'

'Did you hear what happened?' Archie continued, 'She didn't want that disco to play so she took a jug of water and emptied it all over the fuse box for the electrics that work the three pin plug set-up. Shorted the lot out and of course they couldn't do anything about it until that dried out. So the disco couldn't play at all. Proper upset the young 'uns. Lot of people didn't know that Annie's always been a dab hand with electrics, can change a fuse, anything like that. She worked in a factory assembling electrical gadgets during the war and afterwards worked for a local electrician in his shop at Lowestoft. You can't beat her on amps and volts.'

'Well I never. I saw her go off with a jug of water.'

'That ain't all. She went and locked herself in the toilet and wouldn't come out. Was there until eleven o'clock. When people banged on the door she kept saying she hadn't finished. There was lots that were desperate and there was nothing for it but to go outside behind the hall. Weren't so bad for the fellows but a bit rough on the women – you remember what strong winds there were that night. Of course, Annie thought that was a hell of a joke. She would. She's pulled that prank before. Even now there's more go in her than half a dozen of the young 'uns put together.'

Archie turned to go and looked back for a final comment. 'I'll tell you one thing. Them in heaven is goin' to properly have to watch their electrics when Annie gets there, and I hope they've got more than one toilet too.'

The Goose and the Spitfire

TIME WAS when a country house or cottage without a hen run was the exception. A higher standard of living and easy availability of eggs and dressed poultry on supermarket shelves had reversed the situation by the nineteen nineties. During the Second World War and in the immediate post-war period of austerity and rationing, backyard and garden livestock was common.

In addition to chickens many cottagers had a pig which was reared on scraps; or rabbits, ducks, geese and turkeys, the last named usually fattened with the Christmas dinner in mind. In fact, the festive bird on most Christmas dinner tables in this village was then reared not far from the diners' back door. Those residents who plied a profession in one of the nearby towns usually knew somebody in the village who could provide a bird; many backyards that had a plentiful supply of household scraps or access to animal feedstuffs often fattened two or three birds with an eye to this market.

During that period a very upmarket architect named Gilford lived in one of the large country houses just off the village street; Victorian grandeur erected by a retiring member of the Raj. The Gilfords were not the kind of people who kept chickens. Even in those austere days they dressed for dinner and had a housekeeper, cook and a maid. They were definitely the most upper class family in the village, with two of their four daughters at Roedean or some similar elite educational establishment.

The Gilfords had very little contact with ordinary folk round about and it was only occasionally that they would be encountered walking in the village street. It must be said that, although on a higher plane than we lesser mortals, Mr and Mrs Gilford would always initiate a cheery salutation of 'Good morning' or 'Good afternoon', which was in contrast to their snobbish daughters who passed by without a word.

We suspect that the Gilfords saw the farming fraternity as uncouth and kept at a distance, so I was surprised to see Mr Gilford drive his Daimler into the farmyard one bright spring morning. He went to the front door of the house – which must have come as a shock to that portal which was rarely disturbed. Everyone else, even those aspiring to be thought gentry like the Ludington-Witts, went to the back door.

My curiosity, or downright nosiness, drew me to the side of the house to eavesdrop but it was not possible to make out what Gilford and Guv'nor discussed. After the Daimler had departed the Guv'nor called me. Gilford had decided that in view of the current shortages and rationing it would be wise to fatten a goose for the following Christmas. He was having a run built at the bottom of his garden and could the Guv'nor suggest where he might be able to purchase a suitable gosling? Additionally, could we sell him straw for litter and, if possible, a little tail corn.

The Guv'nor, despite his frequent assertions that he treated everyone on their merit regardless of their supposed social standing, had said he was delighted to help. Someone further down the scale would probably have been told that government rules and regulations made certain aspects of this request illegal. Creep, I thought.

The Guv'nor's purpose in telling me all this was then revealed. If Gilford got his gosling then it would be my job to deliver the requirements in the old farm van. Such employment was not to my liking and I was about to protest when the Gilford's pretty elder daughter was remembered. While she was completely out of my class, there is still pleasure to be had in just admiring: a cat can look at a king, so to speak!

At this time Nasty still worked for us. Employed is a better description, for Nasty was not for working much if he could help it. He had seen Gilford's car in the yard and was, understandably, equally curious. I thought it prudent to say no more than that Gilford was looking for a gosling.

It was probably imprudent to have said even that, for Nasty's face immediately brightened. 'I know where I can get one. Seen some fine goslings a mate of mine has got. Just you tell the Guv'nor to send him to me. Let him know I can get him one.'

I said I would pass on the message although I had no intention of doing so. We all knew about Nasty's "old mates" and the sort of dubious dealings that went on. In all probability the old mate would turn out to be some unsuspecting poultry keeper who would be minus a gosling that had caught Nasty's eye. Nasty knew where this and that could be obtained just a little too often for comfort. His services would be the last I would recommend to anyone.

The following Saturday afternoon the Guv'nor instructed me to take a bundle of straw and a small bag of wheat tailings to the Gilfords. Mr Gilford had just phoned to say that he had acquired a gosling. At least he wouldn't be swindled by Nasty, I thought.

As instructed, the requirements were loaded and driven up the back drive of the Gilford's house. I was met by Mr Gilford who asked if I would carry the straw and grain to the pen which was at the far end of the garden, tucked out of view behind the greenhouse. Austerity or not, the Gilfords were not going to advertise the fact that they were fattening a goose to any posh friends that visited. If that was the intention, they obviously had a lot to learn about geese and their vocal abilities.

'We purchased the gosling from one of the men who works for your father,' Mr Gilford announced as we walked towards the pen. My heart sank; obviously Nasty could not wait for his offer to be passed on. The thought of what he might be able to charge this well-to-do gentleman was too much for his avarice which spurred him to make a direct approach before anyone else got a look in. Typical. The only redeeming factor was that when I reached the pen the gosling appeared to be hale and hearty. Knowing Nasty it could just as easily have been on its last legs; more than one ignoramus had been conned into buying some fast expiring creature from Nasty.

'The man who works for your father, what is his name? He did not tell me.'

'He is called Nasty.' Then, seeing the doubtful look on Mr Gilford's face, I tried to explain. 'Everyone calls him Nasty. He doesn't mind. He's always gone by that name. To be honest I've forgotten what his proper name is.'

'How very strange. Very strange. However, he tells me this bird is from a very fine pedigree strain.'

This sounded just like the rubbish that Nasty would trot out to anyone who was ignorant of the subject. I could just visualize him holding forth. But I refrained from telling Mr Gilford the truth that Nasty was the biggest rogue in the district.

'The gosling has been named Gabrielle. My two youngest daughters think it is absolutely darling.'

I said a polite, 'Oh yes,' and thought it time to depart. Gabrielle! What a name for a flipping goose. Then, what could you expect when the Gilford girls all had posh names – Cecily, Alicia, Angelica and Hermione. The two youngest were about eight and ten years old, I guessed, attending private schools as weekly boarders. The Roedean pair, or whatever the establishment was called, were 15 and 17 and only seen in the village during holidays.

During the half dozen visits I made over the following months to deliver goose fodder to the Gilfords, I learned that the name of the bird was changed to Gabriel, back to Gabrielle, and then back to Gabriel again. Sometimes I saw the housekeeper, more often the gardener, who must have been well paid as he drove out from town each day to pot and plant. One can understand his appeal to the Giffords, his use of the Latin names for plants. When I admired the bed of petunias he corrected me with unmistakable disdain; 'No, that's Solanaceae.'

During the summer holidays I was fortunate enough to encounter the delectable Hermione, the pretty eldest daughter. Her rather aloof attitude towards me was accepted, for as I have said, she was out of my class. On reflection, her upbringing had already bestowed a certain air of superior sophistication, even though she was not yet 18, my age at the time. With her sisters she was cooing over the goose and it was obvious the girls viewed it more as a pet than a Christmas dinner. This impression was reinforced next time a delivery was called for. The girls had returned to boarding school and the gardener was relieved as they had been letting the goose out on the lawns, where its voracious appetite was only equalled by the frequent discharge of residues which he had to clear up.

About ten days before Christmas the Guv'nor instructed me to take a wooden chicken crate and collect Gilford's goose. Mr Gilford had been on the phone and asked if we could find somebody to kill it. The Guv'nor said Rue was an expert at wringing the necks of geese – a job that certainly needed expertise. Mr Gilford did not want the execution to occur on his premises because his daughters were very fond of the bird. He had also arranged for the local butcher to dress the carcass, so would we deliver the corpse there? Would we collect the bird early in the morning before the daughters were up and about?

Admittedly, I did not hurry that Friday morning and the Austin Seven van was only firing on three cylinders when started, so a plug had to be changed. Even then, one didn't expect the gentry to be around at 8.45 am, which was about the time I arrived in Gilford's back drive. It was going to be no easy matter getting that damned great goose out of its pen and into the crate. To aid my task, the goose had not been let out that morning and remained in its low hutch at the end of the pen. I was about to undo the trap door in the top of the hutch when there was an agonised cry of, 'Stop. Leave it alone.' I turned to see Hermione running towards me with Alicia, the 15 year-old, close behind, and further back towards the house Mrs Gilford.

Somewhat taken aback, I did not know what to say or do as Hermione threw herself across the top of the hutch. 'Go away you murderer! You are not taking Gabriel. Go away!' Alicia had joined the chorus. 'Yes, go away you horrid lout. You're not going to kill Gabriel.'

Having overcome the initial shock I was able to protest, 'I'm not going to kill it. Your father just asked me to take the bird away.'

There was a chorus of, 'You're not going to. Gabriel is staying here.'

Hermione must have found that her prostrate position on top of the rough wooden hutch was uncomfortable for she slid back on to the ground. As she did so her skirt must have caught on something, for I was suddenly looking at stocking tops, suspenders and an area of bare thigh before the skirt fell back into place.

I have never been able to decide if my having an eyeful was apparent to Hermione and the catalyst of what happened next, or if it were simply a boiling over of her anger about the destiny of the goose. Before I could say another word in my defence Hermione came for me, arms thrashing, belligerence in her eyes. Fists thumped into my chest as I staggered backwards and as I raised my arms to fend off the blows I became aware that Alicia was also lashing out at me. I retreated backwards under this assault of flailing arms, which was accompanied by the most obscene abuse I have ever heard from female lips.

'Stop it girls! Stop it this instant. Stop it!' Mrs Gilford, like the US cavalry of the movies, had come to the rescue and saved me from the indignity of turning to flee. The blows stopped but the abuse did not. I again tried to plead that I was only doing what their father had requested, but was shouted down. Hermione was shaking with rage. Talk about a spitfire.

'You had better go. At once!' Mrs Gilford said it as if I were the one who had offended. There were no apologies for the unprovoked onslaught, not that the blows caused much hurt. Nor, while I was putting the crate back into the van, was there any reprimand from Mrs Gilford for the language her daughters had used. Perhaps they received a good rollicking after the van had limped out of their drive. Alternatively, perhaps Anglo-Saxon four letter words are part of the curriculum at finishing schools for prospective debutantes. All I know is that if a council house woman had heard her daughters use such invective she would not have hesitated in giving them an almighty cuff round the ear.

I related my experience to the Guv'nor and he laughed so much he nearly choked on his shredded wheat. He couldn't keep it to himself, the rotter, and soon everyone on the farm was pulling my leg. That evening Mr Gilford phoned to say that his daughters were so upset he had decided to keep the goose as a pet.

To be honest, I recall feeling decidedly humiliated by the incident and only brightened when, three days after the fracas, the bobby appeared in the yard with the news that Gilford's goose had been stolen. The gardener had gone to let the goose out of its hutch only to find the bird departed. From the bobby's questions to me I wondered if the Gilfords thought I had a hand in this as an act of vindictiveness. Even so, it made my Christmas to think those awful girls had lost their stinking goose.

On New Year's Eve the Guv'nor told me to call at The Anchor and ask the landlady to tell Billy Fogget, the molecatcher, we had a problem on one of the meadows. A jolly, flirty woman, she chatted for a while as there was no one else in the bar. As I left she turned to go into her kitchen and said, 'Well, I must go and mince up the rest of the Christmas goose and make bubble and squeak. Nasty got us a lovely bird; best I've had for years.'

There was nothing unusual in Nasty wheeler-dealing in poultry or looking after the landlady at The Anchor, whom he obviously fancied, judging by the attention he paid her. But I suddenly had my suspicions. Even if the Gilford goose were right at the bottom of their garden it would still require someone who knew exactly what he was doing to take the bird without it kicking up a row. And Nasty was one of those on the farm who had delighted in teasing me when the Guv'nor had told all and sundry about my being set upon by the two schoolgirls.

Nasty may have been light-fingered and devious, but he could also be very cowardly. I tried my usual ploy on the next working day, 'The bobby was looking for you yesterday Nasty. Said something about wanting to know where you got that goose you let the landlady at The Anchor have.'

Nasty's reply was decidedly defensive, 'That were one I reared myself.'

'You always said you didn't like rearing birds. Too much trouble.'

'I don't tell people all I do,' he muttered as he walked away.

Next day Nasty didn't turn up for work. In my view a sure sign of concern that he might encounter the law. When he did return to work his excuse was a bad cold. I would have continued to tease him if, while we were cutting a road hedge on the high meadow, the bobby had not cycled by with no more than a nod of recognition.

'You've been havin' me on, you young bugger,' Nasty hissed when the bobby was out of sight. I laughed, 'I still bet it was you that pinched the Gilford's goose.'

'Don't you 'cuse me of bein' a thief. You know I'm honest.' He didn't sound very convincing or very cross.

There is one more short episode connected with this story. Some time in the following spring I was in the village street and passed Mr Gilford talking to another man. Gilford called after me that he would like to speak for a few moments. I waited until he said goodbye to the other man and he approached. 'I wish to apologise for my daughters' behaviour last December. What occurred was not told to me at the time. I am afraid my eldest daughter seems to have inherited the family temper.' My response was to say it was quite all right and that I realised the girls had become very fond of the goose.

That was my last contact with any of the Gilfords before they moved to salubrious Surrey in the late 1940s. What became of them I know not. The incident related is the only occasion in my life – so far – that I have been attacked by members of the opposite sex. Funny how one's attitude to events changes with passing years; it's now awe for the memory of Hermione's magnificent anger.

The Big Bet

Before television took its toll of traditional rural evening entertainment, betting was a popular pastime among old mates met for quaffing half and halves. Not on horses, the pools or the usual recognised games of skill and chance, but on local events and self-generated challenges, often trivial, sometimes complicated.

As examples, these could be as varied as guessing the size and sex of someone's expectant bitch's litter, the precise number of sheep in Honker Clark's flock that had just been turned out on High Fields Park, and riding a bicycle seated back-first from The Anchor to The Wheelwright's Arms without falling off. This latter was actually achieved by Nibby Teggert, which was not an inconsiderable feat as the distance is a mile and a quarter and a steep downhill stretch is involved; not to mention that he had already stowed several pints of bitter before accepting the wager. The wagers were almost always for pints of beer.

There was a foursome of regular drinkers at The Lamb who were particularly renowned for challenging bets. They were generally looked upon as loners or Shadow Men because of a preference for keeping to their own little group and not being part of the "everyone's a good fellow" situation at The Anchor or The Wheelwright's Arms. Around mid-century, the time of which I write, the three village pubs were decidedly different in character. The Wheelwright's Arms in the village street was patronised by most classes and had a lounge, saloon and public bars, plus a snug and a taproom. Because of its position it drew a fair passing trade. The Anchor, being situated in a hamlet a mile outside the village, had few strangers drop in and was the most popular hostelry where locals were concerned. They said it was the preference for the brewery that owned The Anchor, but the fact that the draught beer was always a little cheaper there than that at The Wheelwright's Arms had more to do with it, and the popular landlord at The Anchor made sure it stayed that way.

The third pub, The Lamb, was even further from the High Street, situated on a quiet road that runs to Great Longham; one rarely found more than a half dozen or so drinkers present, even on a Saturday evening. All were locals who chose to drink there because of the quieter atmosphere or because they liked John May, the landlord for thirty years or more. Of course, there was no living to be made from the pub; it was merely a supplement to May's regular employment as carpenter for Fennie, the builder. The Lamb survived being "tarted up" for longer than any pub that I know in this district. The single public bar had a scrubbed white brick floor and wooden bench seats round the wall and must have looked just the same at the turn of the century.

The foursome who regularly patronized The Lamb were Tommy Riddlestone, Jack Markwhite, Briar Smith and Slippery Eley, all of this parish. Tommy Riddlestone occasionally drove his brother's coaches on the school run or WI outings, although mostly he fetched and carried in his old Morris van for poulterers and butchers in the district. Jack Markwhite was something of an odd job man and dealer, although his most notable activity was thatching stacks and buildings for farmers. Occasionally he would help out the regular thatchers. Briar Smith was a jobbing gardener and, as told elsewhere, acquired briar stocks for rose graftings. Slippery Eley (the origin of whose nickname is obvious) was the only one of the four with regular employment, working for the River Board as a hand labourer. Slippery was reputed to be the most expert poacher in the district. There were several men who poached when they saw an opportunity but Slippery made poaching a professional hobby. And it was this prowess that became the subject of the foursome's most famous bet.

Although these men were then in their late forties or fifties, some

of the challenges dreamed up were more to be expected of youthful pranksters. Many bets were never taken up, such as the proposed seduction of the barmaid at the pub in a nearby village who was renowned for her halitosis. Another non-starter was the midnight switching of the milking herds of two neighbouring farmers. There were many similar dares that did not come off.

One spring evening the foursome were seated in their favourite alcove in The Lamb discussing the reported prosecution of some townee amateur who earlier in the year had been caught red-handed with a partridge by the Great Longham Hall gamekeeper. Slippery had been unwise enough to boast that the keeper would never have caught him in the circumstances involved. One of the others suggested they should put it to the test, and after further contemplation and discussion Slippery was bet that he could not cross from the road bordering the eastern edge of the Great Longham Hall estate to the road on the western side, about a mile and a half, without being apprehended.

During following drinking sessions the bet was developed and refined and finally agreed. The other three bet a five-gallon barrel of best bitter that Slippery could not complete the trip with his dog without being caught. The event was to take place on the next Saturday afternoon and had to be completed before dark. To ensure Slippery did not pull any tricks like doubling back and going round the roads he had to cut down a piece of white sheet that could be seen almost in the centre of the farmland suspended on a pole to scare birds from a recently set maize strip.

To keep an eye on things further, Tommy Riddlestone approached the vicar of Great Longham and asked if he and two friends might go to the church tower on Saturday afternoon to do some sketching. There would be a note in the offertory box as a mark of appreciation. Riddlestone had done a few jobs for the vicar in the past and permission was granted.

Great Longham had a small population and the Church was pleased for any financial support it could obtain. Even so, the vicar had difficulty in believing such a refined interest as sketching was the reason for this request. From the top of the church tower one had a commanding view of the whole of Great Longham Hall estate that lay in the valley, making it an ideal vantage point hopefully to follow Slippery's progress.

None of the three who had wagered a whole barrel of beer against the poacher's skills of concealment thought him able to carry off the feat, but to lessen further the chances of the beer being won an anonymous note was sent to the keeper advising that a man had been overheard in a pub telling friends that he intended to raid pheasants' nests on the Great Longham estate on the next Saturday afternoon in late June.

Although the estate gamekeeper kept a regular everyday check on his kingdom, late June was not poaching time and there was always the possibility that he would not be about that Saturday afternoon; but the note would surely see that he would be. Slippery was informed that the note had been sent and protested that it was a dirty trick. I suppose he could have declared the bet invalid at this stage but pride probably held sway. The bet was on.

At 2 pm on the dot, Slippery Eley and his lurcher dog slipped out of the back of Tommy Riddlestone's van at the road gateway selected as "start". While Riddlestone, Smith and Markwhite headed off in the van towards Great Longham church, Slippery climbed the gate and disappeared into the woodland skirt that bordered the estate. From the cover afforded he looked to see if the keeper were anywhere in view, Slippery having previously observed the lie of the land and planned his route.

The Great Longham Hall estate was roughly a convoluted rectangle of some six hundred acres. One of the longer sides bordered the river and the other the crest of the valley hill where woods and parkland surrounded the Hall, and the small hamlet next to the church. There were water meadows along the river and between these and the parkland was a broad stretch of cultivated fields, mostly carrying crops of wheat and barley. An odd copse was dotted among the arable fields, as well as a few farm tracks. Both parkland and water meadows were too open for Slippery's enterprise, whereas the arable fields were mostly partitioned by hedges and ditches flush with spring growth. These would provide the cover Slippery required.

Slippery Eley was light and lithe – no more than 10 stone and five and a half feet. Small featured, his balding head was rarely exposed. His cloth cap even remained in place when drinking in The Lamb. For this escapade he wore an army jacket and trousers, while on his feet was a pair of plimsolls, so stained that one would hardly recognise that they had started out, when new, as white. Stuffed sacking pads were tied with twine to his forearm and knees as he anticipated that to win his bet most of the journey would have to be crawled.

The first obstacle was a 15-acre field of wheat that was not bordered by ditches on either its higher or lower boundaries. The crop was well advanced and more than high enough to conceal a crawling man and, fortunately, it had been sown so that the rows ran with the valley, the direction Slippery wanted to go. After a little investigation from the security of the woodland strip a drill wheeling was found where the distance between adjoining rows was much more than the normal seven inches. Another quick look for the keeper, a whispered word to his dog to stay at heel, and Slippery was off into the wheat on all fours, like a greased fox. Once he was gone there was no sign, not even a crushed blade of wheat, to tell where he had entered.

The secret was not to break the stems of the crop and only to place hands and feet in between the rows, a slow and precise task, to say nothing of tiring. Slippery's movement would have been hard to spot from 10 yards away on a still day but with the advantage of a soft westerly coming down the valley the crop was in constant if gentle movement and one could have passed within a few yards and been unaware of Slippery's presence.

It was a warm afternoon and frequent rests were needed, but good progress was made. During one of these rests when getting towards the far side of the field, Slippery chanced to look over his shoulder at his dog and nearly had a fit. The animal had a cock pheasant in its mouth! The bird was unharmed but Slippery knew that the moment it was released it would fly away making its alarm call, and that was the last thing he wanted.

The solution came quickly to mind. Squirming round, Slippery took strips of leaf and bound them tightly round the bird's bill. He then pressed forward until he finally reached the edge of the crop. After a careful look to see that the coast was clear, he scrambled into a ditch, took the pheasant from the dog's mouth and bound its bill with grass and then set the bird down to run one way while he and the dog scampered up the ditch in the opposite direction as fast as they could go. Slippery knew the binding would soon come loose.

Fortunately he was able to cross over to another ditch running east-west and was several hundred yards from the pheasant when it was eventually heard flying chuntering away.

Although it was necessary to remain hunched, it was a relief not to crawl and some of the ditches, having been well maintained, were quite deep. After following one beside a hedge that separated a field of sugar beet from one of beans, another bout of crawling was necessary to cross a long narrow field of winter barley that ran from the water meadows a good way up the valley hill. Here the crop had been sown in the opposite direction from which Slippery wanted to take, making undetected crawling far more difficult. If it had not been for the breeze constantly rippling the already eared barley, the relatively short distance, about sixty yards, and the apparently still absent keeper, Slippery would not have gone that way. The alternative was safer but involved a considerable detour by ditch, hedgerow and copse.

This time the dog was sent ahead; no more collecting birds. A typical lurcher and long-tutored in the art of silent and obedient stealth, it seemed almost aware of its master's intentions before they were signified by prods and whispers. The dog slid ahead of Slippery, no more than a tail's length, often faster than he wanted so that it frequently had to be arrested by its appendage.

Taking a final rest before reaching the other side of the field, by looking up Slippery could see the trees in the copse nearby. He became aware of noises close to him. Immediately alert and straining to peer ahead over the dog, he could see movement through the green barley stems. At first he thought it was an escaped pig, but very quickly as the sounds grew in volume he recognised ardent human passion. The dog had started to wag its tail vigorously. Between the copse for which Slippery was making and the barley field ran a farm track which was also a public footpath. Two lovers had obviously diverted into the barley as cover for their activities.

Slippery immediately went into reverse. The dog was less inclined to follow and had to have a hefty tail pull. Once a few yards back Slippery turned and crawled quickly with the rows of barley up the hill as fast as he could go. He reckoned that while passions were roused the lovers would be oblivious to other sounds or movement, but once spent they might be more on their guard.

After a suitably safe distance Slippery turned at right angles and made his way to the edge of the crop. A peep up and down showed the track empty. No sign of lovers or keeper. He quickly crossed the track into the copse and, once secluded behind nettles and willow herb, made a more exacting observation of the fields around.

The first thing that caught Slippery's eye was the keeper's white Ford van parked way up the farm track, a good half mile away. There was no sign of its occupant. Slippery was concerned about that; it was essential to know where the enemy was.

Then he hit on an idea which he hoped would produce the keeper and divert his interest. Softly moving down the copse until he could hear the faint chatter of the lovers in the barley, he took up a stone and hurled it in their direction. He expected that thus disturbed they would eventually stand up and probably be spotted by the keeper, wherever he was. Slippery did not wait to see the immediate result, slipping quietly out of the other side of the copse into another concealing field of wheat, here to rest a while and drink from a flask.

Meanwhile Riddlestone, Markwhite and Smith were sunning themselves on top of Great Longham church tower and wishing they had something better than cold tea to quench their thirst. So far they had seen no sign of Slippery's progress and rarely took their eyes from the fluttering piece of white sheet which he was to cut down on the maize patch. They were briefly distracted from this when two figures were observed on the farm track near a copse. Briar Smith produced his aged telescope and announced that it was a man and a woman. The interest of the three then centred on identification of the couple and from whence they had suddenly appeared.

It was at this point that steps were heard in the tower and the vicar rose out of the trapdoor. There was a hasty grabbing of sketchpads and pencils which no one had so far bothered with. Jack Markwhite had asked his son, who had done well in art school, to start a sketch of some landscape for him, Jack having no artistic skill himself.

When Markwhite opened the pad he was confronted with a drawing of a well-formed female nude but, being blessed with a quick mind, he told the vicar the drawing was of an angel and he only had to put on its wings. The vicar said he had never seen such a well developed angel and was surprised a trip up the tower gave such inspiration. As the other two had nothing to show the vicar felt his suspicions about the purpose of the trio's visit were justified; they were definitely not up there sketching. Seeing the telescope he was concerned that it might be a case of Peeping Tomming until Briar invited him to look at another church across the valley and he realised that one could do little peeping with such a feeble instrument. After the vicar departed they noticed that the piece of white sheet had been cut down. Even though they stood to lose a barrel of beer the three men were quite cheered by the sight.

Slippery was now bent low along ditches on the last half of the estate crossing. It had been necessary to detour a little from his preferred track to cut down the bird-scaring piece of sheet on the maize patch, and as the keeper was still nowhere to be seen he concluded he must be in the woods at the top of the hill. This allowed Slippery to become a little more adventurous and to cut across the top of one of the higher water meadows, using a thick hedge as a shield.

He was about halfway along when he suddenly saw the keeper with gun and dog in the next field walking up the hill from the river, a totally different area from where Slippery had assumed him to be. Slippery collared his dog and sank into the depression beside the hedge that was once a ditch but had long been stamped in by cattle. He could only hope that the keeper kept walking in the direction he was going, for if he came into the meadow Slippery would surely be seen. The minutes dragged, for Slippery dare not raise his head to see. He heard an approach and thought the game was up.

He could not have been more shaken than when a large wet warm tongue slapped against his face and his nostrils were invaded by an overpowering stench of chewed cud. An inquisitive cow was licking him. He dare not do anything to dissuade the animal in case it was startled, and that might attract others. It was a case of stoic endurance as the tongue continued to investigate his face. He prayed the cow would not start licking the dog, which might not be so passive. Next the animal was trying to nuzzle off Slippery's cap and it became a tussle to hold it in place. Eventually, having found nothing it considered palatable, the cow moved away. Slippery could not have been more relieved. Even when he saw the keeper had continued on up the hill it was but an anticlimax in contrast.

With his attention concentrated, Slippery had not really been aware that the sky had clouded over and that rain threatened until an odd spot or two descended on him. Now he had only two fields to pass; one via a long straight ditch and then a comparatively short crawl across another field of wheat to reach the boundary road at the agreed gateway. Slippery was beginning to feel a little smug until he saw the keeper had about turned and was coming straight towards the gateway of the field he was in. There was no time to run back down the ditch as he would surely be seen.

Slippery chose the other alternative, the pipe ahead under the gateway. He judged it to be about two feet in diameter. Dog first, and then Slippery, arms outstretched. His concern was the keeper's dog. Would it investigate the pipe? Fortunately it did not and he heard the keeper pass. Slippery remained in the pipe for fifteen minutes until he could be certain the keeper was well away, then tried to wriggle backwards, only to find that his jacket rucked up and jammed him.

After further goes he would have attempted to crawl right through if it had not been that he could see the far pipes were slightly dropped. The thought of being stuck even more firmly did not appeal to him. Instead he managed to inch his jacket up over his hands and head, finally pulling it free, his uncomfortable position not helped by a small trickle of water that was now coming down the pipe. Outside, the clouds had really opened up.

After several minutes Slippery managed to extract himself from the pipe, put on his jacket and set off once more. He was getting wetter by the minute. The keeper was nowhere to be seen but Slippery could not risk crossing the last field to the road in the open, and he was beyond making lengthy detours with the risk of encountering the keeper again.

So once more it was down on hands and knees, although with less care than before. The wet wheat was no shield from the rain; if anything it helped to saturate his clothes. All Slippery could do to keep up his spirits was to think of the barrel of beer that should be his reward. Hearing passing traffic, he knew he was close to his goal.

He raised his head above the canopy and there, parked on the other side of the road gate, was the keeper's white van! It was the most demoralising situation, yet there was nothing for it but to lie low until the keeper moved on.

The rain had long ago driven the watchers from the top of the church tower. Only once during the whole afternoon had they seen Slippery and that was when he briefly slid across the gateway between two ditches. In Riddlestone's van they set off to park beside the agreed gateway on the far side of the estate, only to find the keeper's van there already with the keeper inside having a quiet smoke. Thus, they had to go on until a place could be found where the keeper's van could be kept under observation.

The keeper, like most pipe smokers, was in no hurry over his enjoyment. He had probably long given up the tip-off of a poacher after pheasants' eggs as a hoax or a misheard story. His wife did not have the evening meal ready until 7.30 so there was no urgency to get home.

When the keeper's van finally departed, Slippery had been lying in the wheat field for a good half-hour. It was an exceedingly sodden bet winner that Riddlestone and company dragged into the back of the van. Slippery even declined a celebratory drink and was taken straight to his home, where his wife was told he had fallen in the river.

In fact, as a result of his exposure that afternoon, Slippery went down with pneumonia. His mates, thinking that he would be in no fit state to dispose of the beer he had won, decided that they had better do him a favour and drink it before it went off, despite The Lamb landlord's kind offer to take the barrel back. Slippery recovered and they bought him a new barrel. He also received many free pints from those who congratulated him on his feat. He said he needed all that beer to try and get rid of the taste of cow cud.

There were others who thought the escapade infantile and more suited to the Boy Scouts than to grown men. Even so, the old boys in the pubs round here still talk of the Big Bet.

Papers' Predicament

MANY PEOPLE find Harry Newson's stories crude or coarse. Despite the inevitable exaggeration introduced whenever he gets into full stride, what he relates is based on truth. Like many countrymen of earthy background he sees no bar to discourse on subjects that more refined folk would consider highly indelicate. Take the unfortunate happening to Papers Pendle, the circumstances of which I recall vaguely, but which old Newson, of course, was able to relate in full detail.

The occasion was when he found me battling to remove a steel drum lid that had become impaled on a wedge-shaped cultivator tine. The tine's pointed head had penetrated the sheet metal easily enough, but it was a different matter when an attempt was made to separate the two. The wide heel of the pointed head could not be forced back through the sheet metal. I tried brute force with a hammer but failed. The only solution appeared to be either to employ a hacksaw or to back the cultivator into the workshop and burn the lid off with the welder. I decided to give the hacksaw a go. A start was made on the bolts securing the pointed head to the cultivator tine. If the bolt were cut away the pointed head would come off the tine. The metal was hard and only a little progress had been made when a cheery voice behind me announced, 'You got trouble there?'

'Yes,' I said, pausing from my labours.

Old Newson shuffled round to the front of the cultivator and stopped to get a better view of my problem. He closed one beady eye and then prodded the offending lid with his walking stick. Finally he drew himself up, raised the peak of his cloth cap with his left hand sufficiently high to scratch his forehead with his thumb and proclaimed, 'Yes, you have certainly got a hard one there. That's just like what happened to Charlie Pendle – "Papers" they called him; surely you remember he? Moved to Hintlesham after he sold his paper business. Happen he's still there. I ain't heard he's pushin' up the daisies yet.'

'Yes, of course I remember him. Can't be that long ago he gave up his papers,' I reminisced, for once appreciating some diversion from a difficult task.

'Blast boy, that were a good 15 years. You don't realise how time fly when you're busy. 'Course, he had a lot of boys deliver the papers round here but used to do out Longham way himself. There were a lot of talk about him and some of them women in the council houses over there.'

'I understood that .....'

'Yes, tha's where he got into trouble.' He interjected with accurate judgement, 'That must have been about the early part of the nineteen sixties. Yes, I reckon tha's about right – about '62. Difficult to remember when you've put as many years behind you as I have.'

I noticed old Newson had placed the point of his stick firmly on the ground in front of him and was now leaning forward on it with both hands so that it took some of his weight. A stance I had observed before when he was about to hold forth.

'As I was sayin', he used to deliver the papers out Longham way himself. Took some time too, 'cause he was always a'mardlin' and drinking cups of tea. Proper owd gossip he were. Wonder he sold any papers, considerin' he spent so much time tellin' the owd gals what was in 'em. Anyways, one hot summer mornin' he's comin' away from some woman's place after a cup of tea, puts his foot on the left pedal of his bike as he goes out of the gate onto the road, and just as he is a'swingin' his leg over the saddle his front wheel hit a small pothole he hadn't noticed. That give such a jolt that his left foot slipped off the pedal and he come down wham on the saddle so hard that one of his testimonials gets pushed right through a crack in the leather.'

'Painful,' I winced.

'Well, that were his own fault. I reckon he'd had that trade bike since the twenties and that saddle leather were old and stiff. That had cracked open along the top where them ventilation holes are but Papers hadn't done nothin' about it. Just askin' for trouble, and him bein' a hefty fellow too. Anyways, he let out a scream and nearly passed out with him and bike ending up in a heap in the middle of the road. 'Course, thas the tenderest part of a man's body. Something painful if they get knocked about. Thas why the Good Lord tucked them out of harm's way down there. He hadn't reckoned on a darn fool like Papers though. Well, two or three of the owd gals round there heard him holler and came runnin' out. The one he'd been suppin' tea with get there first and find Papers a'moanin'. 'Course the first thing she tried to do is pull the bike off him but he only holler more. So then she sees this bulge of grey flannel under the saddle, as I said, that were a hot day and all Papers was a'wearin' is his shirt and a baggy pair of grey flannel trousers. One of the other old gals comin' up the road calls out, "What's the matter?" Her that's tryin' to pull the bike off yells so the whole street can hear, "Paper's got one of his dilberries wedged in his bike saddle!" Well, that did it, the doors opened and just about all the owd girls in the road come runnin'. They thought that were a rare joke, cacklin' and gigglin' they were. Weren't no laughin' matter were it?'

'Certainly wasn't,' I agreed, pausing again from my sawing.

'Poor owd Papers, he's in agony but he say to one of the women, "Don't just stand there a'garpin', push it back gentle like." And what do you think that darned old woman say? "I daresn't touch that, wouldn't be proper. What would my husband say." I ask you, here's a fellow in agony and all they's worryin' about is what their husbands might say. Typical of those women ain't it? When Brigadier Venables' wife had that nasty accident with the top drawer in her kitchen dresser, Bertie Bull the gardener didn't worry about what his wife would say. No, he went straight in to the rescue when he heard her squeal. And a gentleman too; "I'll turn my head and won't look ma'am," he say. Mind you, didn't have to look did he with her great .....'

'Yes, I know all that,' I interjected, 'but who did get Papers free?' The tale of Bertie Bull and his act of gallantry with Mrs Venables' bosom had been related by old Newson so many times I almost knew it by heart, and I didn't want to hear it again.

'Well, I was just a'goin' to tell you,' he continued unperturbed. 'Down the road come a fellow from the local garage in a little pick-up lorry. He has to stop 'cause Papers and his bike is still in the middle of the road. "What's goin' on?" he asked. The owd women say, "Ah, you're just the feller we've been lookin' for."

'So he take a look and have a go but every time he tried to push it back through the saddle Papers holler out with pain. "Tha's no good," says the garage feller,"that'll never go back and tha's starting to swell. That'll have to be cut away." Cor, when Papers heard that, "No no no" he hollered. "Not you, yer darned fool," says the garage man. "I'm talking about the saddle leather."

'Well, the garage man get out his shut knife but then he reckon tha's a job for a doctor so he scratch his head and then he suggests he undo the bolts that hold the saddle to the bike frame so they could get the bike out of the way. He gets his spanners and sets to work. 'Fact, he manages to unbolt the saddle from the frame as well and all tha's left attached to Papers is the leather. Mind you, while he's doin' it them damned owd women keep a'shoutin' out to anyone who come along that Papers is just havin' his nuts undone. They still thought that were funny, stupid bitches. Finally they got the bike out of the way and Papers to the side of the road. Then the garage man discovers that none of them owd women had thought to phone for the doctor. He properly give them a bollickin' he did. There were nothin' for it but to run Papers straight to hospital in his pick-up. So they all lift him in the back and off he goes. When the garage man got to Emergencies he tries to explain what the problem is but he don't know the right medical words. Anyways, a nurse goes outside for a look and she ain't none too pleased at first. "Another pervert!" she say.

'Of course the garage man put her straight on what happened and there weren't no problem after that. The nurse cut the leather off and they kept Papers in for a few days. Well, that swelled up something bad, not as large as Cummy Smith's did when he got the mumps, but a rare size, poor devil. Trouble was all the suspension were strained and so they had to give him a little net bag to support it. Just like them you get your oranges in at Tesco's nowadays. After he got home people was always askin' him how his fruit were.'

'Did he ever ride a bike again?' I enquired.

'Not as far as I know. And 'course, he were no good after that, if you know what I mean?'

'What?' I didn't understand what he meant at first.

'He were no good. He were knackered you might say.' I thought old Newson had surprised himself with his pun, for he burst into mirth.

'You're as bad as those council house women,' I scolded.

'I weren't a'laughin' at that, I was laughin' at you. You've just hacksawed right through that cultivator tine as well as the bolt.'

That I had!